TALES OF NASH

by Ann Worthington

Published 2020

Printed in the United States of America
Print ISBN: 978-1-951490-52-2
Ebook ISBN: 978-1-951490-53-9

Library of Congress Control Number: 2020905860

Publisher Information:
DartFrog Books
4697 Main Street
Manchester, VT 05255

www.DartFrogBooks.com

For my family

ACKNOWLEDGEMENTS

A special thank you to my sweetheart Mike Hurlbut for your infinite love and support. Your optimism makes the sun shine on a cloudy day. I also appreciate the early comments and encouragement from Bruce McCandless III. Your questions and enthusiasm convinced me to keep writing. And thank you to Ruthe Spear and my sister Amy McCoy for providing advice and insight during the writing process.

CHAPTER 1

NOW

The plaintive wail of a siren catches my attention. It reminds me of a bird of prey circling high above a wounded animal, contemplating the kill. I shiver as the hair on my arms stands on end. I hold myself tightly to keep from trembling. *What did I just do?* The mournful alarm grows louder, closing the gap between us as it approaches the hill near the old logging road. I suck in air on rapid, shallow breaths. My heart pounds, begging to escape my chest.

I don't have much time, so I look around frantically, wondering what to do. If I had a choice, I would fling open the door and flee into the woods. I could run to Drift Creek and try to make it all the way to the coast in a day. That fantasy doesn't linger, though. Life as a fugitive wouldn't suit me. Besides, I summoned the police, so I have to stay and meet my fate. I can't call and vanish. That would be cowardly, and I promised myself I would be brave.

I scan the room as the cops outside move closer with every passing second. A table, chair, newspaper and cup occupy the space. I wonder if I should get rid of the water, but decide to leave it. The scene looks more natural with the half-empty glass. I already cleaned up the blood on the floor and the wall. I hurled the empty bottle into the forest, and buried the rags deep in the garden under the broad squash leaves. I'd returned the shovel to the shed, and flushed the latex glove and plastic bag down the toilet. *What did I forget?* I need to wash my hands. Dirt is wedged under my fingernails. As I stare at my grubby fingers, my innards churn and I retreat to the tiny bathroom, thinking I might vomit.

While I'm standing at the basin, a red glow flashes in the yard, like a strobe light piercing the flimsy curtain. The sirens are now mute, but the uniforms move carefully and methodically, closing in on their mark. I can't turn back, run away, or hide. I peek out the window and see the officers, their guns drawn, focused on the door. The blood drains from my face, and a few beads of sweat dampen my forehead. *Okay, take a deep breath. It will be fine.*

As I try to calm the woodpeckers in my stomach, a loud banging startles me and rattles the rickety house.

"OPEN UP! POLICE!"

I inch toward the door, taking a final look around. The body is slumped in a chair in the far corner. A trickle of blood stains the side of its head. I hold my breath and open the door.

CHAPTER 2
THEN

Can you describe your life in three words?
My ninth grade English teacher asked our class that question on the first day of school and required us to write about it. At the time, it seemed like a silly assignment, nothing more than useless busy work. But for some odd reason, it stuck with me, and I often contemplated the question at night before falling asleep. In my essay, I had depicted my life as comfortable, boring and lonely. For several years, that description remained accurate and unchanged.

I grew up in North Portland and lived with my mom on a quiet street in a two-bedroom bungalow. The houses in the area all had weathered siding and sagging roofs beneath a canopy of towering trees. Miles of cracked and crumbling sidewalks connected each abode. Tourists admired the St. John's Bridge or visited the park at night, hoping to see a phantom. Kids rode their bikes and skateboards around while old people strolled with their dogs. Several labor unions had their locals on the main street, where donut shops mingled with thrift stores and fast-food joints. The bums in the area lingered at Mullen's, a dingy bar that smelled like cigarette butts soaked in stale beer. Kids like me hung out at the park to shoot hoops and pretend like we belonged somewhere.

My dad named me after Steve Nash, the NBA Hall of Famer, and I inherited a tall, lanky frame, a freckled face, and chestnut brown hair that stuck up in all the wrong places. I would always grit my teeth when one of my mom's friends said, "Oh, Nash looks so much like his father." I wished people wouldn't say that. I didn't want to be cursed by my face.

My dad took off for Alaska to find work when I was in sixth grade. He had trouble keeping jobs, and when he couldn't get hired at the shipyard or on a construction crew, he left without saying goodbye. He might have landed on the North Slope, but who knew? He wasn't the type to call or send birthday cards. We found out last winter that he shot himself in the head with a friend's pistol. I hadn't seen him since I was twelve, so when the temporary hole in my life became permanent, I didn't cry.

My mom worked nights as a nurse in the trauma center of a local hospital. The brutal schedule zapped her energy and fouled her mood. Most days I made sure I left the house before she finished work. Sometimes I saw her for an hour or two after school, before her shift started. I got used to being alone, and relied on Netflix, video games, and cell phone apps for company. If the weather cooperated, I walked to the park to work on my jump shot because I dreamed of playing for the Blazers someday.

I hung out with my buddies, Cecil and Eric. We met the year before in sophomore English, when our teacher assigned a group project on *Fahrenheit 451*. We managed a C on the assignment, but the grade didn't matter much to us because we became best friends. You wanted Cecil on your side because he never backed away from a dare or a fight. He was athletic, and I went to see him play football on Friday afternoons. As a defensive back, he had good instincts about who would get the ball and could change direction in a heartbeat to disrupt the opponent. As I got to know him, it turned out that disturbing the status quo was part of his identity. He scored a week of detention for riding his skateboard on the roof of the gym when they told him "no skating on school grounds."

Eric was the opposite: quiet, laid-back, and a good listener. He didn't judge you by the clothes you wore or the music you listened to. He brought people together by telling jokes and creating internet memes about high school. Making us laugh helped him forget that his dad left, too, but his married a young girl and started a newer, better family. After school and on weekends, the three of us met by the river or at the park. We also played *Fortnite* or *Call of Duty* at my house, and generally got along because none of us fit in anywhere else.

As a sophomore, Eric earned a leading role in the school play, *Twelve Angry Jurors*. My mom and I went to see one of the performances and were impressed with his talent. Eric was courageous and heroic in his portrayal of Juror #8 and convinced me that an accused criminal remains innocent until proven guilty. He joined us for a celebratory dinner after the show and stayed at our house that night, like he did most weekends. On New Year's Eve, we toasted with sparkling cider and watched the ball drop in Times Square. That spring, Mom and I included him in our Easter brunch and silly backyard egg hunt.

But junior year was different. It stressed everyone out. You took harder classes and exams to help prep for college, plus your hormones raged. I didn't have a girlfriend, but I liked following Tiffany's story on Instagram. She went to my high school and posted provocative selfies, which made it easy for me to imagine us together. I wondered how her lips tasted, and if her skin felt soft life velvet. Preparing for college was the last thing on my mind as I waited for her next post, hoping it would display more cleavage. But my advisor put me in pre-calculus. I hated math, but soon learned the punishment for being good at something—you're forced to do more of it.

I liked being outside in the elements, unconfined by four walls. I listened to the wind rustle the leaves and watched birds flutter between the trees. I observed the boats on the river and imagined sailing one to the ocean. My dad taught me how to fish, but the only rod we had was busted. Besides, a film of pesticide scum coated the water, and clusters of dead fish lingered near shore. In my neighborhood, plastic bags, newspapers, and fast-food wrappers danced in the breeze. I could overlook the trash some days, but sometimes it bothered me, and I collected it when I was alone.

I used to like basketball, and played on both the freshman/sophomore team and in an after-school league. I tried out for varsity as a junior, but got cut. I couldn't tell my mom I failed because she expected me to make the team. I was supposed to stay busy and get involved with school activities. Instead, I told her I was a practice player. She congratulated me and didn't question it. When I came home late, she assumed I went to practice. And with her work schedule, she couldn't attend the games anyway.

But she may have still suspected something irregular that fall. I remember when she asked me about going to a home game.

"What time is your game? I'm not working tomorrow."

"I don't play, so who cares?"

"I care. I want to support the team. What time?"

"I don't know. It's dumb. You don't need to go."

"It's not dumb. I want to be there."

"I don't suit up or sit with the team or anything."

"That's okay. I want to go."

"It's a waste of time."

"Nash, are you trying to keep me away? Are you embarrassed?"

"You just don't need to go."

"I don't care that you won't be playing. I'm proud of you."

"That's so lame."

"No, it's not. You work hard. Maybe you'll make the team next year."

"Geez, Mom. You don't know anything!"

Before I said something I would really regret, I stormed out of the house. She didn't bring it up again, and neither did I.

I only played basketball with Cecil and Eric or other loners who showed up at the park. Cecil hurt his knee playing football and quit the team. Eric decided he didn't want to try out for another high school play, so on sunny afternoons, we challenged newcomers to three-on-three or a game of H-O-R-S-E. We would shoot around, smoke a cigarette, and sometimes drink a beer. We passed the time by telling jokes and being generally lazy.

Cecil had a knack for acquiring contraband, and one day in early fall, he brought a toffee milk chocolate bar to share. He said he stole it from his old man.

"Why would you steal a chocolate bar?" I asked, draining a three-pointer from the top of the key. "You can buy one for a buck at the Mini Mart."

One taste and I discovered the allure of edibles. For the next few hours, we forgot about basketball, homework, and our messed-up families. It was exactly what we wanted, but not necessarily what we needed.

CHAPTER 3
NOW

"PUT YOUR HANDS UP! STEP OUTSIDE WHERE WE CAN SEE YOU!"

I don't want to get shot, so I raise my hands in the air, step outside onto the concrete landing, and then descend onto the crushed rock of the driveway. A light fog blankets the trees like a shroud, and mist speckles my face and arms. With the sun barely up, the morning feels more like autumn than summer.

"Keep your hands up. Don't move!"

The cop in front approaches me with his gun aimed at my chest. His partner moves in from the left, grabbing my arm and patting down my chest, waist and hips.

The cop feels something in my front right pocket. "What's this?"

"It's a pocketknife."

"That's a weapon. Remove it slowly."

"It belonged to my grandma."

"It presents a danger," he says, so I reach into my pocket and retrieve it. "Drop it on the ground."

I follow his instructions and drop the knife onto the gravel. The cop kicks it out of reach, then he continues patting my back and rear pockets.

"What's back here?"

"My cell phone."

"Remove it and drop it on the ground, too."

"It might break."

"Hand it to Deputy Davis then."

I pluck my cell out of my pocket and hold it out in front of me. The officer snatches it from me and slides it into his pocket.

"What's your name?"

"Nash Atherton."

"Do you live here?"

"Yeah."

"Is that a yes?"

"Yes."

"Did you call 911?"

"Yes."

"Is somebody else inside the house?" I bob my head up and down, too nervous to speak. "Answer me verbally," says the officer.

"Yes," I say, feeling weak in the stomach. "My grandpa. I think he's dead."

In an instant, Davis rushes into the house. The deputy who stays with me is tall and has a well-manicured beard and mustache. His khaki uniform is unwrinkled, and the star on his chest shines despite the gray weather. He remains erect and alert in anticipation of news from his partner. For a few minutes, we stand like pawns on a chessboard, waiting for the next move.

An ambulance appears on the street and pauses at the driveway, as if unsure whether or not it should stop. I try not to think. I try not to move. I try not to care about anything at this moment. I feel lightheaded and the drizzle plasters my hair to my forehead. A lump occupies my throat. As I clench my teeth to choke back tears, a sudden surge of fear, sadness and regret washes over me.

When Davis steps back outside, he confirms he found no one inside except an elderly deceased male. I wait in a daze, only partly conscious of my surroundings when the words *coroner*, *warrant* and *evidence* reach my ears. Despite the humming and buzzing noises in my head, I also hear something about an autopsy because the cause of death looks suspicious.

The officer standing with me addresses me again. "What happened?"

I stare at him for a moment, blinking a few times before replying. "I woke up, and he was dead."

"Your grandfather?"

"Yes."

"Does he live here?"

"Yes."

"You reported gunshots and a possible intruder."

"Yeah," I say, nodding my head.

"Do you have a gun?"

"No."

"But you heard gunshots?"

"I think so."

"Did you see anyone?"

"No."

"What made you think there was an intruder?"

"I heard the front door slam and footsteps outside."

"Does anyone else live here with you?"

"No."

"Did you hear anything else? Voices?"

"No."

"Did you notice whether anything in the house was missing?"

"I don't know." I inhale purposefully through my nose, clenching my jaw, reminding myself to just answer the questions. *Don't try to explain. Don't offer long rambling responses.* I learned this from watching a television show about lawyers and cops. Holding your tongue reduces the chance of burying yourself under a pile of lies.

As Davis scribbles notes, the bearded officer surprises me.

"So what happened? How'd your grandfather die?"

"I don't know."

He glares at me and presses for more. "Why do you have blood on your shirt?"

I look down at my clothing, but say nothing.

"What happened, Nash? Did you kill him?"

I blink several times and know I can't answer that question. I stand mute, looking at my feet and the ground, amazed that the two are still connected.

"Answer me!" he says, taking a step forward that places his face within inches of mine. "Did you kill him?"

"I'm not answering that question," I sputter as rain drips off my nose and chin. I inhale, swallow hard, and fixate on the ground in front of me. From the corner of my eye, I spy an endless line of ants marching under the house, and I wish I could follow them.

"How did he die?" the cop persists.

"I'm not answering anymore questions."

"You sure about that?" he snarls, still inches from my face. "No more questions?"

"No more questions," I reply, trying to sound confident, but the rain makes me shiver. I am a wounded animal, caught in a trap, terrified of its fate.

The officer takes a step back, narrowing his eyes as he sizes me up. He grabs his handcuffs. "We're detaining you for questioning.

We have probable cause to believe you committed a crime."

When he handcuffs me, he wrenches my arms down behind my back like he's in a cattle roping competition. I lose my balance and stumble, almost ending up face-first on the ground. To my surprise, the deputy holds onto me, keeping me from tasting a mouthful of gravel. I would have imagined that they'd relish the chance to let the forces of inertia and gravity work their magic, but for some reason, he doesn't let me fall.

"You have the right to remain silent. Anything you say can and will be used against you in a court of law. You have the right to an attorney. If you cannot afford an attorney, one will be provided for you."

He continues his monologue as he leads me to the cruiser, pushing me into the back. *I can't believe this is happening.* The cold vinyl stings my wet skin. The smell of stale rubber invades my nostrils. The feeling of being locked in a cage overtakes me, but I can't do anything except surrender to the seat.

CHAPTER 4
THEN

My life changed dramatically in eleventh grade. The lonely and boring parts disappeared, replaced by friends and a social life. I tolerated school during the weekdays and hung out with Cecil and Eric at night and on weekends. While other kids had sports or music or jobs, we had each other.

We met at the park, near a weatherworn picnic table by the basketball court and sampled whatever goodies we got our hands on. Cecil provided alcohol and the occasional edible. Eric brought cigarettes, weed, or a vape pen he stole from his brother. And me? I had pills.

My mom had access to all kinds of narcotics at the hospital, and she brought some home for personal use. She slipped them into the pocket of her scrubs without a bottle or label, then stashed them in a small plastic bag at the bottom of an old cookie jar in the pantry. I sometimes watched her hide them away from the hallway near the kitchen.

My mom also refilled several prescriptions that kept her functioning. She took one before work to stay awake during her graveyard shift. She took another when she got home in the morning so she could relax and sleep. I'm not surprised she got hooked working nights and sleeping days. If I lived my life upside down, I'd need help, too. But she had to keep that job, even if the schedule was brutal.

"I've gotta work on Christmas Eve, Nash."

"Again? I thought you'd have it off this year?"

"No, it pays time and a half. I need the shift."

"Okay, but you'll be home on Christmas morning, right?"

"Yeah, I'll be home, and I'll try to stay awake for breakfast and presents."

"Can we go to a movie after that? Or drive up to Hood to see the snow?"

"Not this year. I need to sleep before heading back to the hospital that night."

"What? You're working on Christmas, too?"

"Yeah, time and a half, remember?"

"That sucks."

"It's not so bad. We'll have time to do something over the break."

"But Christmas will be over."

"Well, I can't help it. We need the money."

"Can Eric come over to hang out then?"

"Sure."

When she had time off, she struggled to keep a regular timetable. Without her meds, she dozed at the breakfast table, watched television all night, and forgot to buy groceries. One time when we drove to see Grandma and Grandpa, she fell asleep at the wheel. We were on the highway and veered onto the shoulder. We lurched down an embankment into the ditch, and a tow truck had to pull us out. Neither of us was hurt, but it scared me. As soon as I got my license, she let me handle the longer drives, but that didn't happen very often.

I spent most of my time with Cecil and Eric. We got together and experimented with our sweets, as we called them, mixing them up and testing different combinations. The pills surprised us sometimes because we couldn't always identify them. Some had a distinctive shape or color, and others had telltale markings. It didn't matter to us, though. We didn't hesitate before playing Russian roulette with an unknown tablet.

"Close your eyes and pick one," I said to Eric.

"How many are there?"

"There are three on the table. You choose first."

"And then chase it with a beer," encouraged Cecil, popping open a can.

"Okay, here goes."

The blissful mix of drugs and alcohol worked like magic, temporarily relieving our boredom and eliminating any pain. We called ourselves The Three Buzzkateers and made silly videos of each other on our phones.

"Give me a truth or a dare," suggested Cecil about an hour later.

"Let me get my camera ready," I replied.

"Pick your poison," said Eric.

"Dare, of course."

"Here's a good one. I dare you to staple this piece of paper to your forehead."

We looked at the small square of paper Eric held in his hand. I went to the kitchen drawer and retrieved the stapler, opening it wide for Cecil. When my phone was poised and recording, we started the game over for the audience's benefit.

"Buzzkateers here with another episode of I Dare You."

I panned the camera from Eric to Cecil, and Eric repeated his directive.

"I dare you to staple this piece of paper to your forehead."

"I got this," said Cecil as he stared down the camera. Then he rested the note against his head with one hand and pushed the stapler with the other. "Shit, that hurts!" he screeched as he jumped around the kitchen like a crazy kangaroo.

"Oh man, that's effed-up," Eric said as we laughed and I posted the video on YouTube. Cecil pried the staple out of his skin, and we howled at the mark it left behind.

"It's my turn to film now," said Eric, grabbing my phone. "Cecil, you're in charge of the call."

"Okay, Nash. What's it going to be? Truth or dare?"

I rarely picked truth because I'd have to admit I fantasized about seeing my math teacher naked or had kissed another guy. I preferred a dare and didn't mind the risk of physical pain. It scared me less than public humiliation.

"Dare," I replied, feeling the strength of the sweets coursing through my body.

"Oh, this is going to be good," said Cecil. He went to the refrigerator and grabbed a bottle from the door. "Get the camera rolling, Eric."

"You're back with the Buzzkateers for another round of I Dare You."

Eric aimed the camera at me, and I tried not to look nervous. I never knew what kind of a challenge Cecil would invent.

"I dare you to drink this entire bottle of ketchup."

"No problem," I replied, smiling for the camera and nodding my head confidently. I grasped the bottle in my right hand and flicked the top up. "Give me a countdown."

"Five, four, three, two, one."

When I heard "one," I tipped my head back and squeezed with all my strength. The salty, tangy, sweet goo filled my mouth and I forced myself to swallow. It felt cold and thick on my tongue and throat, and I gagged only once.

"Look at that boy chug!"

"Keep squeezing!"

When it was empty, some of the ketchup ran down my chin onto my shirt. When I smiled for the camera, the red stains on my teeth made Eric roar. "Watch out for the vegetarian vampire."

All the kids at school watched our outrageous videos. We didn't show ourselves getting high first. We only uploaded the outcomes, particularly the dares. Students I didn't know recognized me and gave me high fives in the hall. Tiffany even smiled at me one day. We also got thousands of likes on social media. We entertained and offended with equal ease, and people commented about what they wanted us to do next. Around Halloween, we carved faces on pumpkins and smashed them in front of the camera. We threw them like a shot put or bashed them with a baseball bat. We shoved them into the side of buildings and launched them from a slingshot.

The pills played an integral part of our antics, and I didn't feel bad about swiping them from my mom. She stole them anyway, and I figured she could always get more. But for some reason, it bothered me to deceive her about basketball. My life used to revolve around NJB, March Madness, and the Blazers. I couldn't believe my mom didn't notice the change. She swallowed my story about competing on the practice squad and stopped asking questions. I guess she wanted to believe I had talent and drive and ambition, and I got used to pretending to be the kind of kid she wanted as a son.

After living the lie for a few months, without any arguments or inquiries, I couldn't admit failure. I wanted to come clean, but what was the point? She thought I was busy, and that's what seemed to matter. The guilt weighed me down though, suffocating me and impairing my judgment. At the time, the story, like everything in my life, seemed totally harmless.

Was it surprising that my introduction to ecstasy was euphoric, a fantastic surprise on a dull December day? Cecil, Eric and I met at the park, but the arctic temperatures forced us back indoors. A stiff north wind penetrated our feeble jackets as we lumbered toward my house. My mom's car occupied the driveway that day, so we changed our plan. Seeing her would mean suffering an inquisition because the school principal had been calling. I'd missed a bunch of classes and was failing another. A counselor also wanted to talk to her about my recent academic dishonesty. We did an about-face and went to Eric's house a few blocks away.

His older brother Carl lived at home, but he wouldn't bother us. We went to Eric's room and unloaded our sweets while Cecil unpacked a fifth of vodka. Eric revealed three edibles that looked like gummy bears, and I had one oblong green tablet.

"That's it? Pretty lame input, Nash."

"The supply is running low. It's all I could get."

"What's up with you lately? Keeping the good stuff for yourself?"

"No. I think my mom suspects. She hasn't been adding to the stash."

"You haven't brought anything good lately."

"I know, but this is morphine. It'll be great."

"Great if you had three, but it's only one."

"You guys can split it. I'll just have a candy and some juice."

Satisfied with our agreement, we each ate a gummy and chased it with a quick swig of booze, then went to the kitchen for a knife to cut the pill. As we argued about which blade would do the job, Carl joined us, eyeballing the pellet.

"Have you dorks ever met Molly?" he asked.

We shook our heads and Cecil replied, "Who's Molly?"

"It's not who, you loser, it's what. Molly is ecstasy. MDMA. THE party drug. You have to try it."

"Have you tried it?" Eric confronted his brother.

"Yeah, I've tried it, you runt. It's awesome. It lasts for hours."

"And you're just going to give it us?"

"Not a chance, but I'll trade you three of these for the one you've got on the counter."

We looked at each other and debated whether to accept. At the time, it didn't occur to me that he recognized the greenie and knew its value. Instead, he'd focused our attention on his supply. If we liked it, he could get us more for twenty bucks a pop. He also said he would barter with me for more of my stash. Eager for a new experience, we accepted Carl's offer.

A few minutes later, a pleasant sensation wriggled through my body, like puppies playing on a roller coaster. We cranked up the music, waved our cameras around, and danced like bumper cars at a carnival. The evening unfolded like a psychedelic dream, and the colorful sounds enveloped me like a satisfying hug. As the hours passed, we laughed, cried, and shared our darkest secrets. Eventually we crashed, and woke up the next morning with headaches, dry mouths, and multiple bruises.

We skipped school that day, and I had to explain to my mom that I stayed home sick. I needed her to call the attendance office and excuse the absence. When I forced myself to vomit, she thought I had the flu. She didn't need to know the truth, and I got the day off to sleep. Even after surviving a brutal hangover, I knew I would take that trip again.

CHAPTER 5
NOW

As a child, I imagined riding in the back of a police car would be an exciting adventure. I visualized speeding down the road with the siren blaring and the radio squawking about crimes in progress. I don't think that anymore, and I keep my head down. I focus on the dirt and grease that stain my blue jeans and the blood on my shirt. I don't want to look out the window and risk seeing somebody I know. I am ashamed to be sitting with my hands behind my back. Alone behind the tinted glass, I brace my feet on the floor of the car and struggle to remain upright through the hills and curves of the rural roads.

Rather than daydream during this drive, I should prepare for what comes next. Detention. Unfortunately, I'm familiar with that, but not at the police station. At school, detention means staying after class and doing homework—barely a punishment. I don't know what today will be like. *Will I be in a cage with a bunch of people? Will they hassle or try to intimidate me?* I know not to talk to anyone without a lawyer. *But how do I get one of those? Should I call my mom?*

But instead of focusing on those things, my mind drifts to a memory of my dad. He got arrested once when I was five or six years old. We were driving back from Grandma and Grandpa's house on the interstate. Dad was behind the wheel, Mom occupied the front passenger seat, and I rested in back. It might have been dark because I remember seeing the flashing red lights before hearing the siren.

When Dad pulled over and the officer approached the window, I sensed trouble brewing.

"Why were you going so fast?" my mom hissed through clenched teeth.

"I don't know! I thought I was keeping up with traffic," argued my dad.

"Oh crap! Get rid of this," my mom groaned, sliding a few empty bottles under her seat. "You know we can't afford a ticket!"

"Do you think it smells like beer in here?"

My mom sniffed the air while my dad held a hand to his mouth to check his breath.

"Quick, open all the windows."

Before we could air out the car, the officer loomed next to my dad, and requested his license and registration. He then asked if Dad had been drinking. After hearing a negative response, he stated the vehicle smelled like booze and ordered him out of the car. I was too scared to turn my head, and tried to peek out the corner of my eye. My mom sat frozen in her seat. Several minutes later, the patrolman returned and said he was arresting Dad for driving under the influence. He had failed a breathalyzer test and was going to jail. Mom needed to take over and drive home.

My dad had to spend the night in jail, but they found a lawyer who could get him out the next day. After that ordeal, most of my parents' arguments revolved around their drained savings account and Dad not doing anything to replenish the coffers.

And here I am, handcuffed in the back seat of a police car, just like my dad. I wonder what thoughts ran through his mind all those years ago? *Did he feel scared? Was he worried someone would see him? Did he think he'd shamed his family?*

I shake my head to clear the memory. I don't want to dwell on that. I'm headed to the police station and need to stay tough. Besides, my dad should not have been driving after drinking. Everyone knows that's illegal. He brought that misery on himself, and he endangered his family in the process. Although he never talked about the incident or apologized, I hope he felt sorry for his actions.

I look up because we make another sharp turn, and I sense a change in the landscape. We're near the coast now, and a different memory floods my brain. I was a little older, maybe seven or eight, and I remember camping on the beach with my dad. Mom stayed home so it could be a guys trip. We packed like we were going to Grandma and Grandpa's house, but ended up near the dunes. When the tide was low, we grabbed shovels and spent hours digging for clams in the cold, wet sand. I couldn't dig fast enough to capture the mollusks, and I marveled at how a creature with no arms or legs could avoid my scoop.

My dad managed to collect a few, but he spent most of his time sitting on a rock drinking. When it started to rain, we retreated to the tent and ate stale graham crackers for dinner. Mom didn't pack us anything for the trip because she knew Grandma would have everything for the evening meal and s'mores. She didn't know Dad changed the plan, and when we stopped earlier in the day, he only bought beer. With the wood too wet for a fire, we couldn't even boil the dozen or so clams we had scavenged from the sand.

Despite the disappointment of that trip, I never told my mom, and I remain captivated by the beauty and contradictions of the Oregon coast. Angry waves batter placid rocks and crash against serene sand. Howling winds whip stately trees and taunt tranquil shore birds. I haven't been to the coast in weeks, and I won't go today. It may be a long time before I feel the sand between my toes or taste the salty air on my lips.

CHAPTER 6
THEN

I hung out with Eric a lot more that winter, and Carl made sure we had whatever we needed. Cecil showed up sometimes, but he had a new girlfriend and spent more evenings and weekends with her. Eric and I had each other, and we entertained ourselves by getting high and watching television, making videos, or just staring at the ceiling. We felt like brothers and talked about our dads. They were missing from our lives, but not absent from our thoughts.

I didn't even pretend to play basketball anymore. My worn-out ball became flat from neglect. I sold my prized Dame 5 shoes at the consignment store after Christmas so I could buy drugs. I doubted I could even run up and down the court, and had no interest in layups or free throws. What was the point? I spent most of my time figuring out how to make a different kind of score.

After a couple months, my once amusing hobby became a vicious habit. To make it work, I stole money and drugs from my mom. I got wasted and forgot about school. I failed a few classes that semester, and lied to everyone, including myself, about my messed-up life. My teachers wanted me to talk to the counselor, but I ignored their requests. As the weeks passed, I kept digging a deeper hole as I tried to recapture the initial thrill of partying.

In a short time, I owed Carl a bunch of money and doubted I could ever catch up on the payments. Despite the looming debt, he often introduced me to new ways to get high, and I took to them like an eager lab rat.

"I should make you pay for a hit of this stuff. It's primo."

"I don't have any money."

"Then you don't get to try it."

"Fine. I don't need it."

"Yeah, but you want it. I can tell. Everybody wants this."

"No, that's okay."

"But this is the best. Don't be a wuss; take a hit. You'll see."

"You sure? I can't pay."

"This one's on the house."

He gave me free stuff, but resented my inability to pay. He threatened me, warning me to bring money or he'd break my fingers or bash my skull. Most of the time, I went out of my way to sidestep everyone except Cecil and Eric. They had similar troubles and clung to the same sinking ship I was on.

The school sent the cops over sometimes because of truancy, but we managed to stay one step ahead of them. My mom tried to intervene, but I avoided her and simply stopped going home, except to steal money or her stash. She tried to reach out to me, to reason with me, to talk to me, but I resisted. More than once, she begged me to get help, but I ignored her. In a futile attempt to interrupt the cycle, my mom even changed the locks on the house to keep me out. But in my desperation, I punched through a window to get in.

I traveled a dangerous path that winter, a slippery slope that spiraled downhill. I was headed for disaster, but felt powerless to stop or change direction.

During the spring of my junior year, I challenged my friends to the ultimate dare. Over the break, when other kids worked, traveled, or looked at colleges, Cecil, Eric and I shared a total binge weekend.

"Cecil, are your parents of out of town this weekend?" I asked.

"Yeah. They're leaving Saturday morning."

"Great. Party at your house," said Eric.

"Yeah, but let's keep it small."

"Sure. How small?"

"Maybe just us?"

"No girls? Is it a party without girls?" I asked.

"Maybe a few girls, I don't know, but don't broadcast it, okay?" said Cecil.

"If there aren't going to be any girls," said Eric, "let's bring everything we've got and get crazy."

"That could work. I've got plenty of booze and some edibles."

"And I've got a full pen. What about you Nash?"

"I've got a dozen pills saved up, but I want to get some coke. Can Carl get us some?"

"I think so. He can get whatever we want."

We met at Cecil's on Saturday afternoon and wasted no time starting the party. We had saved up for the trip like a holiday or vacation, and extended our credit with Carl to the maximum in order to make it all happen.

That night brought a blur of noise and silence, color and blackness, pain and joy, unicorns and demons. We ran around the neighborhood half naked, punched mailboxes with our bare fists, pissed in the doorway of Mullen's Bar, ransacked the shelves at the Mini Mart, and put out cigarettes on each other's skin.

I passed out and ended up in the emergency room after someone's dog found me in their front yard, face down in the mulch and dead leaves. I couldn't open my eyes at first, but recognized I was in a hospital. Straps secured my arms to the bed, while the beeps and blips from various machines kept me company. Some kind of tube invaded my throat and made communication impossible.

As I lay like a corpse, an invisible brute tortured me. It pounded my head with a hammer, then burned my throat and stomach with acid. I twitched and jerked as strange images and noises flooded my head. I shivered and cowered, too weak and afraid to confront the beast.

In that vulnerable state, I thought about the three words that used to describe my life and decided comfortable no longer fit. Miserable, pathetic or depressing fit better. But a bright spot hovered in the corner of the room. Before I opened my eyes, I knew my mom lingered nearby. I recognized the subtle scent of jasmine from her perfume. Despite my failure as a son, she still cared about me. She held my hand, kissed my forehead, and told me everything would be all right. I felt stronger knowing she hadn't given up on me. After a week of sweating, trembling and sobbing, I faced the fact that I had a serious problem—a problem I couldn't solve on my own.

I reluctantly talked to the police about the crimes I'd committed. While recovering in the hospital, they arrested me and charged me with possession of drugs, vandalism, theft, and disorderly conduct. My mom hired a lawyer, and I pleaded guilty to those misdemeanor offenses to avoid jail time. Because I didn't have any prior arrests and remained hospitalized under supervision, the judge gave me one year of probation and community service. Some of the nurses called it a slap on the wrist.

A counselor named Larry met with me to discuss my behavior, and why I chose to get high. It didn't help that my best friends used drugs, and when I hung out with them, I used, too. But I couldn't blame Cecil and Eric. They never forced me. My meetings with Larry were awkward at first. I didn't say much, but he kept pushing. *How do you talk to a stranger about your flaws, secrets and fears?* He asked a ton of questions and forced me to answer.

"When did you start using drugs? Why did you start using drugs? What problems did you try to solve with drugs? Did you feel good using drugs? What are some alternatives to drugs?"

As I tried to figure out the correct responses, I wondered if insecurity haunted me like he suggested. Did I somehow feel inadequate while sober?

And it felt stupid to discuss basketball, but Larry urged me to talk about everything.

"How did you feel when you didn't make the team?"

"How do you think I felt? Horrible. Like a loser."

"I understand your reaction; failure can be difficult to handle, but it was just one thing in your life."

"It was NOT just one thing. At least to me. Basketball was everything. It was my life, what I dreamed of doing."

"Do you feel like you turned to drugs to cope with the disappointment?"

"I don't know. Hanging out with my friends was fun. Getting high was fun."

"Do you have any friends who are sober?"

"Not really. But I mean, we weren't always wasted."

"No? Not all the time?"

"Well, lots of times. It was fun."

"Yes, I've seen some of the videos on your phone. Your mom shared them with me."

"I was a Buzzkateer, and that meant something."

"What did it mean?"

"That I had friends."

"What else?"

"That I was cool."

"What does being cool mean to you?"

"It means people liked my videos."

"You felt popular or valued by that?"

"Yeah, I guess."

"And that helped you forget about basketball?"

"Some of the time."

"So getting high was a distraction, but you still felt bad about not being on the team."

When I thought about it later, I realized I had found an entertaining alter ego. I felt confident and powerful when people liked my videos. They thought I was fearless, and sometimes I believed it.

But then there was the issue of my dad. Of course Larry had more questions about that.

"How old were you when your dad left for Alaska?"

"Twelve."

"Had your parents divorced?"

"I guess. Dad didn't live with us anymore."

"Did he talk to you about why he was leaving?"

"No. He just left."

"Did your mom talk to you about it?"

"No. I don't know. Maybe."

"What do you mean, maybe?"

"She told me he was going to Alaska to find work. I didn't think it was forever."

"How did you feel when he left?"

"Fine, I guess. I didn't see him much anyway."

"You weren't angry or sad or upset?"

"I don't remember."

"You're blocking, Nash. You've got to deal with this and feel it, even if it hurts."

"I don't know what you're talking about."

"It hurts when someone leaves, especially without saying

goodbye. Only after you feel it and accept it can you move on."

I sat quietly for a while, my brain scrolling back to that time in middle school. Larry broke the silence.

"What are you thinking?"

"That it still hurts."

"What hurts?"

"When you get left behind."

"Can you describe how you felt?"

"No. I'm not good at that kind of stuff."

"Give it a try. What comes to mind when you think back to that time?"

"Why does it matter?"

"It's going to have an effect on you, even if you don't want it to."

"Well, maybe it didn't affect me?"

"I think it did. Come on, Nash. Tell me."

"Screw you! Why do I have to talk about it?"

"You felt angry. You still feel angry."

"Yeah, he freakin' left, and didn't even have the guts to say goodbye."

"Good. Keep going."

"I wasn't worth sticking around for." Tears welled up in my eyes. "He brought his friend's stinking dog to Alaska, but he didn't bring me."

"That's it Nash. Let it out. It's okay to feel and express that anger."

"But how will that help?"

"When you feel the pain, if you can embrace it and meet it head on, maybe you won't have to use drugs to escape it."

I thought about that later. Did I use drugs to avoid the loneliness and pain of being abandoned by my dad? Under the influence, I didn't need a father. And any lingering thoughts that he didn't love me, or that I drove him away, evaporated like steam rising from a boiling pot. I cried during those sessions, shedding more tears than I had during my entire life.

Throughout my hospital stay, the doctors delivered bland advice about getting healthy and recovering from addiction. I used to skip breakfast, have a soda or candy for lunch, and then get wasted instead of having dinner. They lectured me about dietary guidelines and the benefits of eating fruits and vegetables to repair my damaged organs. When the limp green beans and mushy peas appeared on my tray, I threw them in the trash. When they loaded half my plate with broccoli and sweet potatoes, I launched it across the room. I begged my mom to bring me a cheeseburger and fries, anything that would taste good.

"You have to help me. I'm starving. The food here sucks."

"You'll be fine. It's good for you. Try something new."

"I don't want new. I want something that tastes good."

"You need a healthy, balanced diet, like the doctor said."

"Just one slice of pizza? That's not too much to ask."

"You need to eat what they bring you."

"How about this? If I eat everything on the tray at lunch, you bring me Taco Bell for dinner?"

"No, Nash, you need fruits and vegetables."

"Why do you want me to suffer even more?"

"Stop being so dramatic. The food looks good, and you need it to get well."

They said my body would heal itself if I gave it a chance. Maybe they were right, but what about my brain? What about my desire to get high? Would I ever be free from the temptation to use?

One day when I detected the faint smell of cigarette smoke on the hospital cleaning lady, I begged her to get me a smoke. She said no at first, but I persisted. The next day, she let me take a hit from her Juul. Just one inhale and the nicotine spiked my brain, sending instant calm throughout my body. I counted on those meetings and paced up and down the halls looking for her. When I didn't see her for a couple days, I was furious and punched an orderly in the gut when he tried to steer me back to my room. They strapped my arms to the bed again, and some guy in a business suit stopped by to talk to me.

"You just assaulted a hospital employee. We need to call the police and file a report."

"Please don't do that. No police," I begged. "I'm sorry."

"You're violent, and we're not equipped to handle that type of behavior."

"It won't happen again. I promise. I just lost my head."

"It better not, or I will get the police involved. The orderly doesn't want to press charges, but this is your only warning."

"Okay," I say, hanging my head.

"What set you off anyway?"

"I don't know. I'm just going crazy here. I need fresh air or something."

"We'll add this incident to your medical file and discuss it with your doctor and therapist. But now that you're done with detox, it might be time for an outpatient program."

The prospect of getting out of the hospital motivated me to behave. I ate my vegetables and talked to Larry. As I struggled to figure out alternatives to using drugs, I also opened up to my mom about the last six months.

"I didn't want to disappoint you and tell you I got cut from basketball."

"Geez, Nash. I'm disappointed, but not about basketball."

"I know I shouldn't have lied, but I can't believe you didn't notice."

"I was busy. I wish you had just told me."

"It seemed easier to make up a story."

"And look where that got you. We could've worked it out. You know that."

"I guess, but I didn't see it that way."

"You know you can be honest with me."

"And what would you have said if I told you I got cut from the team?"

"That I was sorry to hear it."

"That's a lie. You would've yelled at me and told me to work harder. I know it."

"I might have been upset, but I try not to yell. We could've looked into other options."

"Like what?"

"Like the Boys & Girls Club. Don't they have a league?"

"Not for high school kids."

"What about your coach? He might have known about other leagues or suggested a team manager position. Or you could've gotten a part-time job."

"But I wanted to play varsity, and I wasn't good enough."

"Not everybody is, Nash. It's a tough lesson to learn, but you're good at other things."

"Like what? I can't think of one thing."

"Give it some time. You'll figure it out. But your choice to take drugs was dangerous. You could've died."

"I know, but you take them every day and seem fine."

"I'm not fine, though, and I set a terrible example. It's dangerous for me, too. I promise I'm going to get help and stop."

"But I don't know if I can stop. It's all I think about."

"It's going to take a lot of hard work, but I know you can do it. We both can."

"Sometimes it seems like it would be easier to be dead, like Dad."

"I hope you don't mean that. What happened to your dad is not your fault. It's not my fault, either. He made the choice to end his life."

"Were we that bad that he wanted to get away from us?"

"Of course not. We didn't drive him away, and I don't think there was anything we could have done to make him stay."

I sat quietly for a few minutes, pondering my mom's statement. *How could she be sure there was nothing we could have done?*

"When I partied, I didn't think about Dad leaving. I could forget, and it was like he didn't exist."

"You and I may never forget, but we have to deal with the anger and grief we're feeling. I'm going to talk with a therapist about it. You should, too."

"I've talked with Larry about it. He said I tried to escape from those feelings, but all I did was bury them."

"Maybe I did the same thing."

"I just wish I knew why Dad left."

"We'll never know why, and I feel terrible that I didn't talk to you more about it. That was a mistake. I avoided talking about your dad. I guess it hurt me, too."

"Not knowing is harder than knowing."

"I agree, but we can't do anything about it now. And when I think back to my other mistakes, it was wrong to keep drugs in the house."

"You tried to hide them."

"I wish I had caught on sooner."

"It wouldn't have stopped me, though."

"But I still feel guilty about contributing to your problem."

"Why did you bring them home anyway?"

"I don't know, Nash. I guess I thought I might need them sometime."

"You wanted a stash, just in case."

"Yeah, just in case. But I got rid of it, and I'm going to get help."

Overwhelmed by the initial recovery, but with daily support from my mom, the nurses, and Larry, I managed to make it through each day and focus my attention on the future. I had a chance to make amends and start anew. Maybe I would come up with some different words to describe my life.

I avoided one problem, however, and refused to discuss it during my recovery. Carl. I didn't tell anyone about him, that he supplied most of the drugs, and that I owed him a bunch of money. As much as I wanted to be truthful with everyone, and as hard as they pressed for details, I couldn't throw him to the wolves. You don't do that to your best friend's brother. And even though he exploited my drug use, my instincts told me to keep my mouth shut. I learned from the movies that nothing good ever comes from ratting out a dealer.

I vowed to find a way to repay my debt to Carl. I knew him pretty well, and he could be a reasonable guy. He scared me though, so I kept that information to myself and gambled on being able to make a deal.

CHAPTER 7

NOW

When we arrive at the county sheriff's office, only three other cars occupy the parking lot. The deputy helps me out of the car, but keeps me handcuffed. He knows I might make a run for it if he liberates my limbs. The rain has stopped, and low clouds obscure the sky, clinging to the tree branches like shadowy ghosts.

We step inside a nondescript building to start the paperwork: name, birthdate, address.

"You've been detained as a suspect in the death of Fredrick Atherton. Are you ready to make a statement?"

"No. I want a lawyer."

"Do you have someone in mind you'd like to call?"

"No."

"Do you have money to pay for a lawyer?"

"No, but my mom might."

"Do you want to call her then?"

"Not really. She's at work."

"Then I suggest you call the public defender."

"Who's that?"

"They're lawyers who are paid by the state. They work for clients who can't afford private representation."

"Okay, but I don't have my phone anymore."

"You can use this phone," says the deputy, pointing to the clunky black apparatus next to him. "The number is printed on the desk."

He releases my handcuffs, and I rub my wrists, staring at the ancient device. It looks a lot like the one at Grandpa's. *Who should I call? My mom, who is probably at work, or these public defenders?* After a brief internal debate, I lift the handset and punch in the numbers.

"Hello, Office of Public Defense Services. How may I help you?"

"Uh, hi. I'm at the sheriff's station and need a lawyer."

"I see you're calling from the Newport office in Lincoln County. Is that correct?"

"Yeah, I guess."

"Have you been arrested?"

"Um, no. They brought me in for questioning, but I don't want to answer any questions without a lawyer."

"Okay, what's your name and address?"

"Nash Atherton. I was living at 3400 Drift Creek Road, near the Siuslaw National Forest, but my home address is in Portland."

"That's fine. What's your occupation?"

"I'm a high school student."

"How old are you?"

"Seventeen."

"Okay. Full-time students qualify for free or reduced cost representation."

"Good, because I don't have any money."

"And why did the sheriff bring you in for questioning?"

"Because my grandpa was dead."

"All right. Someone will be assigned to your case and will contact you at the sheriff's station."

The phone goes dead, so I hang up, uncertain about the exchange. *What kind of attorney works for clients who can't pay? Are they even real lawyers?* I just hope it's someone with experience.

As I ponder whether I have other options, the deputy addresses me again.

"Are you wearing a belt?"

"No."

"Remove your shoes then. I've got slippers for you."

"What? You want my shoes?"

"Standard procedure. No shoelaces allowed in the cage."

I hand him my canvas Converses and realize I've never worn slippers. I slide them on my feet, and the extra fabric looks awkward sticking out behind my heels. The officer bags my dirty sneakers and places them behind him on a shelf. Then he stands.

He grasps my arm and walks me down a long stark corridor to a holding cell. As we proceed into the bowels of the building, I don't see or hear anyone else. I consider bolting for the exit, but know that would be stupid. Too many obstacles block my path. Besides, the slippers might trip me up. I'm stuck, at least for now, in this dungeon.

CHAPTER 8
THEN

Grandpa is my dad's dad, and I used to call him Gruff. He had a mess of gray hair and stared at you with piercing eyes and a furrowed brow. He rarely smiled about anything. Growing up, I got to see him and my grandma quite often. They lived in the Coast Range on a large piece of land near Drift Creek. They tended a garden and kept hens. Grandpa hunted deer and elk with a crossbow and fished for cutthroat trout and steelhead. They liked the solitude, coexisting with nature. I remember my dad saying Grandpa relished the challenge of tracking game in the steep terrain and taking aim with his bow.

When my parents lived together, we visited Grandma and Grandpa during the holidays, to celebrate birthdays, and for a couple weeks every summer. We would drive south, pitch a big tent on the property near the creek, and enjoy the wildness of camping. I loved it because I played outside all day and pretended to explore like Lewis and Clark. I floated leaves down the creek, whittled arrows out of sticks, and followed imaginary bear tracks in the woods. I also enjoyed falling asleep outside, listening to the lullaby of the water as it rushed over the rocks, racing for the coast. One time, when it was cold and rainy and I asked to sleep inside, my dad told me no.

"You need to stay in the tent. Your grandpa has nightmares."

"He does?"

"Yeah. He wakes up screaming, cussing, and shaking you in your bed."

"He did that?"

"Lots of times."

"Why does he do that?"

"It's from the war. He can't seem to forget Vietnam."

"That sounds horrible."

"I think it was. He doesn't really talk about it."

"I won't have to go, will I?"

"To war? Not unless you sign up. Grandpa got drafted and had to go."

During our trips, my dad showed me how to fish, and sometimes Grandpa joined us. It was more fun with just my dad, though. Grandpa criticized everything and ordered us around.

"You're wading in the wrong spot."

"Sorry."

"You've got too much slack on that line."

"I do?"

"Stop fidgeting and be still."

"Okay."

"Keep your hook away from those rocks."

"I'm trying."

My dad didn't dare assert himself or offer a conflicting opinion. For the most part, he followed orders like everyone else. One time, near the end of a spring break trip, I was in the yard chasing a chicken, and Grandpa raised an axe, scolding my dad for drinking and complaining too much. I hid behind the shed and watched.

Mom had started working nights at the hospital.

"If you can't get a decent job, at least look after your son!"

"I look after him."

"By drinking and watching TV?"

"Nash is fine."

"He needs more from you. He needs a father."

"Like I needed a father?"

They stared at each other for a moment, while I remained frozen in place. Then my dad spit on the ground and walked away, retreating into the house.

Dad also told me other stories about Grandpa.

"Why is he always in a bad mood?"

"That's just the way he is, Nash, so I'd do what he tells you."

"What happens if I don't?"

"You might end up like me, chopping wood for three hours because I didn't study."

"He made you do that?"

"Yup. I failed a test in high school, and it was supposed to teach me that studying was easier than working."

"But Grandpa seems to like work. He's always out in the shed fixing things."

"He was a machinist at the paper mill for many years. He likes to work with his hands."

"Maybe he'll teach me?"

"Don't count on it."

Grandpa detested highway driving, so they never ventured to the city to see us. "Too many idiots," he used to say. "Everybody's in such a goddamn hurry." Did he mean us or other people? I didn't dare ask.

After Dad left for Alaska, Mom and I still visited and camped at the property. I did my best to stay out of Grandpa's way while my mom and Grandma worked the garden, made jam, and canned vegetables. They stayed in touch by phone, and shared recipes, photos, and gifts during the holidays. Mom invited them to Portland all the time, but they preferred to stay home.

I remember one of our trips to Drift Creek, when just Mom and I visited. I sat in the kitchen eating peanut butter cookies on a rainy day. During a quiet moment, I asked Grandma how she met Gruff.

"He had been discharged from the service and was back in Oregon working at the paper mill. I was a cashier at the hardware store, only a few years out of high school. One day, he came in to buy a wrench. I thought he was handsome, but he didn't say much. He paid for the wrench and left. I didn't give it another thought until he came back to the store every day for a week to buy something. I think he just wanted to see me."

"That's funny. Did he finally talk to you?"

"Yes, but I had to make the first move. I asked him, 'Why don't you take me out to dinner? Then we can talk about something besides the weather and hardware.'"

"Did he take you out?"

"He sure did, and we got married six months later."

Grandma said they bought this property and started a family. I always thought Dad was an only child, but at some point, I overheard a conversation about his older brother, Mark. Nobody talked about him, and I used to wonder why, until Mom told me Mark died when he was ten.

When Grandma passed away, we didn't see Grandpa anymore. Mom talked to him on the phone sometimes and sent him birthday cards, but we gave up camping. It didn't bother me. My mom worked long hours and used her days off to sleep. I spent time with my friends and dismissed camping as an activity for kids.

CHAPTER 9
NOW

As the iron bars clank shut and I collapse onto the cold metal bench, I can't stop second-guessing myself about calling the police. I had several other options this morning, including calling my mom, going back to bed, or walking out and never looking back. *What was I thinking?*

Contacting my mom might have been a good choice. I just talked to her last night, but our conversation had been weird, and I couldn't remember if she was working today. If I had gone back to bed, I wouldn't have been able to sleep. *Who can fall back to sleep with a dead body in the other room?* And walking out? Well, that wasn't really an option, either. If I had a car, I might have driven away, but the truck was old and unreliable. With my luck, it would've broken down before making it out of the forest. Instead, I called 911, and now they suspect me.

I lean back against the tile wall and try to convince myself I'm innocent, but a sick feeling of doubt gnaws at my gut. *They took my pocketknife, but it's clean. Was it a mistake to flush the baggie and the glove? Maybe I should I have buried them in the garden, too. And where the heck did that bottle come from? Am I going crazy, or was Grandpa? He had that gash on his head. I cleaned up most of the blood, but they noticed it on my shirt.* I gaze at the stain and wonder why I didn't change clothes. I could've buried the shirt, too, but I guess I wasn't thinking straight.

It won't take much digging for them to figure out I'm already in the system. I don't remember a whole lot about that binge weekend, but I felt invincible when the party started, then it fell apart. The police report has all the details, and I'm guessing they'll label me a hoodlum or a derelict. They might lock me up before I do more harm. Worse than that, at some point, I'll have to face my mom. She'll be so disappointed when she finds out I'm in jail. I can already see the look on her face, the anguish in her eyes. I can hear the pity and disgust in her voice. And just when I assured her I'm doing well. I admit I've made plenty of mistakes during the past year, but I don't want to go to prison.

I yawn several times, feeling the weight of exhaustion pressing down on me. I need to check out for a bit and clear my head. It's either the floor or the bench, so I choose the latter. I curl up and stretch my shirt up over my face. I find the semi-darkness comforting, despite the harsh conditions. *Try to think of nothing,* I tell myself. My body wants to relax, but my brain wants to reflect. I close my eyes, willing myself to hibernate, but my thoughts turn to Grandpa.

To most of the world, he was stern, rugged, and fiercely independent. He didn't like to ask for help and went out of his way to avoid it. The saying "every man is an island" suited him perfectly. But after living with him for several months, I got to see a different side of him. As I got to know him, his crusty exterior softened, and revealed a surprisingly gentle soul. And once he got to know me, I felt like he understood me. Unlike my dad, Grandpa talked to me. Unlike my mom, Grandpa listened to me. And after a short period of time, Grandpa trusted me.

I drift off to sleep, my mind swirling with thoughts and memories, knowing Grandpa cared about me.

CHAPTER 10
THEN

After several agonizing weeks in the hospital, they released me back into the world. I felt physically stronger and more mentally alert than I had in a long time. Now I just had to stay that way.

The doctors and counselor met with my mom and me to discuss a plan for recovery.

"I suggest boot camp to reinforce the good habits Nash has been learning," said the doctor.

"I don't think we can afford that," replied my mom.

"It's not that expensive."

"Well, not to you, you're a doctor. We live on my income with no safety net."

"Then reform school is probably out of the question, too."

"Yes, insurance doesn't cover those things."

"What about an outpatient treatment program?" Larry chimed in. "They have one here at the hospital."

"Is it a good idea to have Nash hanging around a bunch of addicts?" replied my mom.

"Well, it can be a support system. They're on the same path he is. They help each other."

"I see. And how does Nash fill all the hours in a day during the summer?"

Everyone looked at me, and I didn't know what to say. So far, all the options sounded bad.

"He shouldn't go home and risk falling back into the same routine," Larry replied.

"I know, and I don't want him spending time with his old friends, either," said my mom.

She didn't want me near Cecil or Eric. They both survived the binge but had to deal with the police and their own parents.

"What are you going to do then?" Larry asked my mom.

"I have an idea that just might work."

On the first day of May, without celebration or fanfare, I moved in with Gruff. Mom had told Grandpa about my troubles and suggested the arrangement. She thought a simpler life, with structure and physical labor, might benefit me. Plus, she knew Grandpa needed help since he lived alone. They agreed I would spend four months at Drift Creek, learning about life the old-fashioned way: by doing chores.

"You're moving tomorrow, Nash."

"I know, Mom."

"You should pack a bag."

"I will."

"And bring your school books. Grandpa doesn't have a television or video games. You can focus on passing English and health class."

"I know that."

"We're leaving early, so I want you to be ready."

"Okay."

"And you won't have a car, I'm dropping you off."

"What am I going to do all summer?"

"Whatever Grandpa tells you."

She gave me an old cell phone for emergencies, but warned me she would monitor my use through the wireless company. Not that it mattered; the signal in the forest was weak, and Grandpa didn't have Wi-Fi. My mom had destroyed my old phone, so an ancient flip phone was my only link to the modern world. At that point, according to her, I had three goals. Stay sober, learn the value of hard work, and take responsibility for my life. It sounded just like boot camp.

"Come on, Nash, it's time to go."

"Can't we wait another day or two? Or just not go?"

"No, we had a deal. I told Grandpa we'd be there by noon."

"Why do I have to go? Can't I get a job here and join a therapy group like you?"

"No, absolutely not. You're going to Grandpa's."

"That's so stupid. It's better if I stay here."

"No, it's not. You need to go."

"But why can't I just stay here?"

"Because Grandpa needs you."

"That's crap. You're dumping me there."

"Would you rather go to military school?"

"We can't afford that, so I know it's not an option."

"I might take out a loan to pay for it if you don't get your butt in the car."

"Fine."

"Besides, I need to see Grandpa anyway. I baked him some cookies and want to give him an herbal supplement for his cough."

My plan to weasel my way out of the deal failed, so I resigned myself to enduring a four-month term with Gruff. We drove south in silence with my mom at the wheel.

I considered asking her if she'd quit using drugs, but the words never materialized. Instead, I thought about returning to the Stone Age with no television or computer. I also wondered if Carl would track me down when he found out I'd moved for the summer. I avoided a confrontation with him in the hospital, but now it seemed inevitable. I needed to hide for a while, try to get some money, and cut a deal to pay him back. I had no idea how that might work, and the uncertainty of it all worried me.

I stared out the window as the scenery changed from open highway and grassy farmland to narrow roads that twisted through dense forest. After spending several hours listening to crummy music on the car radio and dozing in my seat, we finally arrived at the property. I saw Grandpa outside in the yard working the soil, and a few scrawny chickens scattered when our tires hit the gravel driveway. I used to feel excited about coming here and exploring with my dad, but this time I felt anxiety and dread. It felt like walking into a classroom at a new school, where you didn't know anyone, but you knew the teacher was mean.

As we got out of the car, Grandpa stopped digging long enough to say hello to Mom and tell me to put my gear inside. I only brought one bag with clothes and my backpack with a few books, so I followed orders, climbed the three steps to the house, and opened the door. The lingering smell of wood smoke and dead fish greeted me as I tiptoed inside the dark musty kitchen. I set my stuff down on the floor in a corner near the table and glanced around. Through the grimy window, I saw Mom talking to Grandpa. He coughed and clutched his chest, and she handed him the plate of cookies and a small package. My mom's nursing instincts compelled her to take care of everyone.

With nothing to do inside, I sauntered back out to say goodbye. Mom got teary and said she'd miss me. I found that hard to believe after all the trouble I'd caused her. I imagine she rejoiced about getting rid of me for the summer, but I didn't say those things. Instead, I put on a brave face and told her I'd be fine. I'd call her next week. As she drove off, Grandpa coughed again, then delivered his first command.

"Grab a shovel, we've got work to do."

"What? Already?"

"Yup, already."

"Shouldn't you tell me what we're doing or show me around first?"

"You've been here a dozen times or more. Has your brain been so fried that you can't remember?"

"No. I know where things are."

"Okay, then. Grab a shovel, and follow me. We're digging a garden."

Although I hadn't been there in years, the familiar sights and sounds flooded my senses. I recalled the silence that enveloped the land, the pungent smell of damp earth, and the infinite collage of green foliage. I also remembered the boss. When we used to visit, nobody argued with Grandpa.

We spent the rest of the afternoon turning the soil, preparing the garden for seeds that would be planted later. The backbreaking work demanded all of my strength, and I struggled from the start. We cut rows, formed mounds, and dug holes. Dirt got everywhere, including in my pants, shirt and hair. Grandpa barked orders every now and then, and I either groaned or nodded, keeping my mouth shut. When we stopped, blisters had erupted on my hands, and my shoulders screamed in pain. I wanted to collapse on the ground, but somehow Grandpa remained spry.

"I can see you ain't very strong," said Grandpa. "It'll take time, but you'll get better. Wear some gloves tomorrow. We got lots to do in the next few weeks."

Great, I thought, hanging my head, rubbing my neck. *More digging, just what I wanted. Would every day be like that? If so, I* might not make it through the week.

"If the weather's good, we start planting tomorrow," he continued. "But it's quittin' time now. We need to have supper."

The mention of food was music to my ears. My stomach felt hollowed out like a bowl. My mouth watered as I thought about tasting a delicious double cheeseburger with onion rings, ketchup, and ranch dressing. Or a couple slices of pepperoni pizza would fill my belly. Maybe I would have a milkshake, too, with Oreo cookies and chocolate. But the sweet melody came to an abrupt halt when I heard Grandpa's next words.

"Get washed up. I made stew."

"Stew?" I blurted out with a sneer. "Can't we go get a burger or something?"

Grandpa turned and looked at me like I'd dropped an F-bomb in church. He narrowed his eyes and furrowed his sweaty, wrinkled brow. I imagined steam erupting from his leathery ears. I braced myself for a tongue-lashing, but to my surprise, he didn't yell. Instead, he kept his piercing gaze on me, frowning as he spoke.

"No. We don't eat out. We eat here."

Before I could reply, he turned and walked to the metal pump in the yard. He worked the handle up and down, and fresh cold water poured into the bucket below. As I watched, Gruff drenched his face and head, letting the liquid drip down his body. He stripped off his shirt and used it to dry himself, then walked directly to the house and disappeared inside.

I stood in the yard for a while and tried to make sense of my plight. There would be no cheeseburgers, pizza, fries, or ice cream: no reward for a hard day's labor, no chance for a smidge of joy after a grueling day. How would I survive?

I don't know how long I stood there, but before long, the mosquitos attacked, so I retreated. I splashed water on my face and scurried for shelter. Grandpa waited for me in the kitchen.

"It's about time. Stew's getting cold."

"Whatever."

"C'mon, try it. I made it with elk meat."

"Eww. Elk?"

"It's good. My neighbor and I got the kill a few weeks ago."

"Sounds appetizing," I said with sarcasm.

"I know it's different from what you're used to, but it's what we got."

I wrinkled my nose and took a whiff of the dish, frowning at the smell. Eventually, I dunked my spoon and gave it a taste. *It couldn't be worse than hospital food, right?* There was a long pause while we chewed and swallowed.

"There are only three rules here," he said. I stared at my bowl without replying but looked up briefly to acknowledge his words. "Work hard. Stay sober. And be honest."

"Is that it?"

"Yup, that's it."

I ate the stew that night, then went straight to bed. I was tired and wanted time alone to consider my options. *Another few days in the garden might kill me. And eating stew every night? Could I somehow talk Grandpa into driving to town for a burger? Or could I call Eric and beg him to rescue me? Or, some night while Grandpa slept, could I steal the truck and vanish from this horrible place?*

I can't explain it, but envisioning a scenario where I escaped the drudgery calmed me down. Crazy as it sounded, pretending I had choices allowed me to unwind and fall asleep. Maybe I was lying to myself, constructing a fantasy to survive, but somehow, I needed to figure out how to get what I wanted from this arrangement.

CHAPTER 11
NOW

When I wake up, I have a crick in my neck and sore shoulders from napping on the bench. I sit up and stretch my back. Did someone pour cement in my arms and legs? I don't know how long I've been here because they took my phone. I wish I had it so I could at least text my mom. The police have probably contacted her by now about my detention and Grandpa's death. Part of me hopes she didn't answer the phone. Nobody wants to get that call.

I don't really want to talk with her right now, but she has to know I need help. If she can hold it together long enough to drive here, maybe she can pick me up. But I shouldn't get my hopes up. She could be at work and not know about Grandpa yet. Or worse, she may want to leave me here or send me to military school. I can't predict her reaction, so I figure the longer I put off communicating with her, the better.

I've got other problems at the moment, like dehydration. I crave a soda but would settle for a drink of water. A stainless steel sink and toilet stand in the corner of the cell, but I'm glued to this spot. *Can fear cause temporary paralysis? Or is this a crazy scene in one of my dreams, and when I wake up, I'll be in my own bed? What a relief it would be if the last year of my life disappeared into the fuzzy folds of my brain like a fading nightmare. But what if I shift positions and don't wake up? This could all be real.* I shudder, squeeze my eyes tightly, and slide down the bench. When I peek, I see the same puke green cage around me.

My swollen bladder demands that I get up, so I stand and stretch my legs. *Thank heaven they put me in here alone. I'd be too scared to pee with strangers staring at me. Ah, that feels better. Can I drink the water from the sink?* It looks suspect because it's mounted right next to the toilet, and the equipment on both looks identical.

I really need a drink. *Where did everybody go?* I pace back and forth and question why I haven't seen anybody or heard anything since they dumped me in here hours ago. I grab onto the bars and look through them at the drab cinderblock wall. They stuck me at the far end of this cave. *The cops better not forget about me like that college kid in San Diego who nearly died after he was left in a cell for days without food or water.*

Try not to panic. I start pacing again. *Take a deep breath and consider the options.* I can yell for help or whistle or scream.

But wait, are footsteps coming this way? I stop to listen and my heart pounds in anticipation. I also hear keys, the sweet clinking of old-fashioned keys on a ring. *I bet that means I can get out of here. I don't belong in a cage.*

A short, thick man in a tan uniform appears and looks at me through the bars. He has dark eyes and bushy eyebrows, like two large caterpillars. He doesn't smile or speak at first, but studies my face for a moment. I approach the bars and see that his name tag says he's called Olvera. He continues staring and this makes me squirm. It takes all my fortitude to maintain eye contact.

When he speaks, the creases around his mouth barely move.

"You ready to talk?"

Startled by his words, I step backward and say, "No." My lips and tongue feel parched and brittle as I clear my throat and attempt to swallow. A dozen thoughts rush through my head, but only one rises to the surface. "I want water," I sputter, my voice cracking a little.

"You got water over there," he says, gesturing toward the sink.

"I want drinking water."

He considers this for a moment and asks again in a low voice. "You ready to talk?"

"No," I say, crossing my arms over my chest and planting my feet.

Olvera frowns, shrugs his stout shoulders, and walks away. I'm left alone again while the once sweet jingle of keys disappears down the hall. My heart sinks as I return to the bench and drop down onto it.

CHAPTER 12
THEN

L iving with Grandpa forced me to get up at sunrise. I resisted at first, and covered my head with a blanket and pillow to block out the light and muffle the noise from the kitchen. "Get up, lazy bones!" Grandpa yelled as he banged on pots and pans to rouse me. Even in my room, I couldn't escape the clatter or the offensive hack of his mucus-filled cough. And without a shade covering the window, the sunlight cruelly interrupted my slumber. Before long, I surrendered because my cot didn't encourage extended lounging. A bargain purchase from the Army surplus store, the faded green canvas sagged in the middle like a lame hammock.

I stalled for time in the kitchen.

"I can't work on an empty stomach."

"Then make yourself some breakfast."

"But you don't have any cereal, and I don't know how to cook."

"I'll show you how to fry an egg and put bread in the toaster."

I pretended to forget things in the house in an effort to delay the inevitable chores. I took multiple bathroom breaks so I could waste time and accomplish less. I worked sluggishly as I daydreamed about getting back to Portland, my friends, and a normal life.

Grandpa tried to teach me about the garden, how deep to plant the seeds and how far apart, but I rolled my eyes and ignored him. Sometimes he would stand next to me and physically show me what to do, like I was five years old. When I messed up or failed to complete a task, he shouted at me, "Stop being an idiot, and pay closer attention!"

I found Grandpa's unpredictable moods and frequent rants frustrating. And he wouldn't leave me alone. How could I do the minimum and slide through my four-month sentence with him monitoring my every move? I didn't care whether the garden had vegetables, weeds or pests. It was just dirt. The chickens didn't need my attention, either. They could run around the yard and find seeds and bugs to eat. And Gruff could screech all day, but I would never, ever clean that coop.

During that first week, I got a letter in the mail from Cecil.

> Hey, Nash. Maybe you heard I'm moving. My dad got a job out in Redmond. I hate it and wish I didn't have to go, but I don't have a choice. The only good thing is I'll be working on a landscape crew this summer so I can buy a car. Eric's been busy working and taking a summer school class. He seems good. Maybe you'll see him. I'll miss you senior year. Your friend, Cecil.

I crumpled up the letter and threw it away. It was just my luck. My friends had jobs and money and actual lives. Not me. I made zero cash and lived like an exile in a run-down shack in the woods with a crazy old man.

One afternoon, Grandpa left in the truck and I searched every cabinet and drawer for something to drink or smoke. I needed to numb my brain and distract myself from the constant thought of dropping everything and leaving. I found several things of interest in the house that day, but only one lousy beer in the refrigerator. It sat tucked in the back like bait, and I debated whether to drink it or not. When I popped the top and the cold, carbonated liquid poured down my throat, I felt instant relief and comfort. A familiar calm softened my brain, and I wished I had five more. But the relaxing effect vanished, and I regretted my decision. I had consumed the only beer in the house and had no prospects of getting more.

I contemplated calling Eric. He could get me something sweet to numb my brain and help me mellow out in the evenings. He could also give me an update on my situation with Carl. I located the crappy cell phone in my backpack, but the battery was dead. I plugged it in to charge and waited for signs of life. After failing to get even a faint signal to make a call, I tried texting. If I sent one to Eric, and if my mom actually monitored the account, I would hear about it soon.

That evening, when Grandpa returned, he inspected the refrigerator.

"Something's missing."

I didn't respond.

"The beer is gone."

Again, I stayed silent.

"Don't do that again," he said as he shut the refrigerator door.

I couldn't believe it. He didn't call me out: no yelling, no scolding, no lecture. I expected a sermon, but Grandpa remained silent and basically overlooked my delinquent behavior.

Deprived of the internet, video games, and television, I thought about cracking open one of the eleventh grade English books I brought with me. I still had a chance to pass the class if I read The Great Gatsby and The Catcher in the Rye, and sent reports on both to my teacher. Instead, I went to bed early, mentally fixated on the secret cabinet behind the door in the kitchen, and the bank statement I found in a drawer while snooping. I wondered what was hidden in that cupboard and vowed to find the key that fit the lock. More importantly, I discovered that Grandpa had almost twenty thousand dollars in a savings account. That night, I fell asleep wondering what it would be like to have that kind of money, and what I might have to do to get it.

Most evenings, after an endless day of work, I sulked about my predicament and refused to help Grandpa with additional chores. We argued about it sometimes, but one night in particular, his request incensed me, and the confrontation that followed spiraled out of control.

"I do the cooking, and if you're gonna eat, you need to help with the dishes."

"If we ate out, neither one of us would have to do dishes," I replied.

"But we don't eat out, we eat in, and you need to do the dishes."

"Fine. I'll do them later."

"You'll do them now."

"If you had a dishwasher, I would, but you don't have squat."

"You got a roof over your head and food on the table, so you better darn well help."

"You call this slop food? I'd rather eat dirt and sleep outside than stay in this dump you call a house."

"Get out then!! Go out and try to make it on your own."

"Maybe I will. Anything's better than being stuck here with you!"

"You ungrateful little punk!"

"Maybe if you weren't so mean, Dad would still be here."

My words stung Grandpa like a whip against bare skin, opening a raw wound. I knew I'd made a mistake the second the venom left my lips. I'd overstepped my bounds by mentioning my dad, and I couldn't take it back. Grandpa wilted like a rose in the desert, and tears dampened his weary eyes. *Where had those evil words come from?* I didn't want the night to end like that, with anger and pain and hard feelings, but I couldn't bring myself to apologize.

After a beat of awkward silence, Grandpa withdrew from the kitchen, and from me. I watched as he walked slowly to his bedroom and closed the door.

CHAPTER 13
NOW

I must have dozed off again. In my sleepy haze, someone nudges my shoulder and I hear, "Wake up now."

I open my eyes and see a woman standing over me, offering me a small paper cup of water. Without thinking, I sit up, grab the water, and swallow it in one gulp. I glance at her smooth, round face. I've never seen a young female cop. I like her brown doe eyes and dark hair pulled back in a ponytail. She reminds me of Tiffany, but older. The nametag on her uniform reads Casey.

"I brought you a sandwich and an apple," she says, setting a square plastic tray down next to me on the bench. "You can use the cup for more water. It's fine from the sink."

"Thanks," I say.

I unwrap the sandwich and take a huge bite. I don't care if liverwurst hides between the slices of bread. I've been here for hours and had no food since dinner last night. As I chew and swallow, I think about last night. It seems like forever ago. Grandpa wanted venison, grilled medium rare, with fresh herbs, mushrooms, and beans from the garden. I had become the primary cook, but he didn't eat. He just smelled the meat and sucked on a few bites before spitting them out.

"You're hungry!" The chirp of Casey's voice snaps me back to the present. "You ate that sandwich in three bites. That might be a record. I'll see if I can get you another one before your lawyer shows up."

"My lawyer?" I say, sitting up a little straighter and taking a bite of the apple. "I have a lawyer now?"

"Yes," replies Casey, turning to face me. "You called for one when they brought you in this morning. It's someone from Public Defense Services. Do you still want a lawyer, or have you changed your mind?"

"I want the lawyer. When will he be here?"

"In about an hour," says Casey, glancing at her watch. "And it's not a he, it's a she."

As I contemplate this information, Casey picks up the empty tray, pivots, and walks out, closing the bars behind her. My lawyer will be here soon. That's good news. They can't keep me here forever. *But do I have to answer their questions?* I need advice about that. And when it's over, I'm going to need a ride. *Should I call my mom? By now she's got to know that Grandpa is dead, and I'm a suspect.*

I return to the bench with a million thoughts racing through my head. They're going to search the house because "things look suspicious." One of the cops said that this morning. *How can an old man in a chair look suspicious?* I guess it's the cut on his head. My lawyer will probably want to know about that. *Should I tell her what happened? Should I tell her that Grandpa and I had argued several days before? That he avoided me and refused to speak to me? That I found his behavior maddening and offensive? And that, until last night, we both remained sullen, too stubborn to have a conversation and resolve our differences?*

Even a patient person might snap under those circumstances.

CHAPTER 14

THEN

The early days of May crept by, and Grandpa and I worked side by side, planting an immense garden. In the evenings, I filled in worksheets for health class, answering questions about nutrition, exercise and reproduction. We never mentioned the accusation that he compelled my dad to move all the way to Alaska, or worse, to commit suicide. I thought about it, but felt too awkward to apologize for my outburst, and Grandpa acted like it never happened.

Instead, we focused on the garden. Grandpa told me what to do and I did my best to comply. We planted beans, broccoli, tomatoes and corn first, then carrots, cucumbers, peppers and squash. We staked the beans, weeded the rows, and built fences to keep the rabbits out. We labored in silence, minding our own thoughts, avoiding any real conversation. I imagined myself as a slave, toiling in the fields for no pay and meager rations. Even doing math homework seemed better than that drudgery.

At night, after dinner, I withdrew to my room and shut out the world. I wished I had my old phone so I could at least listen to music, maybe Khalid or Post Malone, but instead, I endured a chorus of crickets and frogs. Grandpa sat in his chair and read, but I didn't join him. He set out a deck of cards and a backgammon board, but I ignored those, too. I tried to reach my mom by cell, but she didn't answer. Leaving a message seemed pointless. *What would I even say? That everything was fine? That I was doing great?* I could've lied and told her a story she wanted to hear. But what good would that have done? I had traveled that road before, and it was a dead end. It seemed better to tell her nothing than admit the truth.

Besides, I knew if I talked to my mom, I would beg and plead and promise to be good and stay sober if she let me come home. Although I longed for the familiar sights and sounds of my neighborhood, the park, and my friends, the prospect of being in Portland made me uneasy. I had unfinished business with Carl. As much as I detested staying with Grandpa, I feared my mom would cave, and then I would have to face Carl, my unpaid debt, and the likelihood that I'd soon return to drugs.

One afternoon, after several weeks in the garden, I pulled the weeds and wished I could sink into the soil and disappear. I imagined digging a hole and burying myself under the broad squash leaves. Without realizing it, I began sobbing, and the tears and sweat joined as they dripped down my face. I dropped my head into my dirt-crusted hands and whimpered. Grandpa came over to check on me: not out of concern, but most likely to make sure I didn't crush his vegetables.

"What's wrong with you?" he asked sternly.

"What's wrong?" I wailed. "What's wrong is I hate this! I hate being here. I hate working all the time. I hate not having a TV or video games or friends. I hate not having any fun!"

I didn't care if I humiliated myself. I wanted to give up.

When I'd finished my tirade, Grandpa stood there looking down at me, shaking his head in disgust. Then he groaned and stomped away while I sat in the soil, wishing I was anywhere but there. When Grandpa returned, he carried a basket, a large bucket, and two fishing rods.

"Come on, Nash. The garden can wait. Let's go down to the creek and see if anything's biting."

I picked myself up, wiped my eyes, and sheepishly followed him down a barely visible path at the far corner of the yard. We walked in silence beneath a canopy of Douglas fir and western hemlock trees, the forest floor carpeted in moss, sword ferns, and Oregon grape. Soon, the familiar soothing sounds of Drift Creek caressed my ears, just like when my family camped here years ago. I inhaled deeply, smelling the decaying logs and pungent earth around me. As Grandpa refreshed my memory about finding worms for bait and fishing the rocky crags of the creek, I felt more at ease than I had in a long time.

Although Grandpa panted and wheezed after our walk, he seemed eager to fish, and talked in spurts about my first few weeks.

"The garden looks great. We made good progress."

I nodded, and he seemed pleased.

"We've got other projects to tackle, though. I'd like to rebuild the chicken coop and add more fencing around the garden. The roof needs fixing, and if we finish all that, maybe we can go on a hunting trip, bag an elk or two."

Grandpa talked and talked, but I paid little attention. The flowing water had me mesmerized as I cast my line into the shade, attempting to coax a fish out of hiding. As I focused on my line, remembering all the things my dad taught me, Grandpa surprised me.

"You're a big help, Nash. I should thank you."

I looked up, but stayed silent for a while, absorbing the appreciation. It felt good to hear some praise instead of insults for a change. I hadn't done anything good or right for such a long time, I almost felt proud.

"Your grandma Helen was an expert in the garden. She loved tending the plants and keeping things tidy. She would nurture the seedlings and talk to them like they were her children. She said a garden is like a child. You can't plant it and expect it to take care of itself. It needs attention, nutrients and guidance. I really miss that woman. She was the best thing that ever happened to me."

Grandpa paused, moved upstream a few yards, and recast his line. I remained quiet, reverently focused on Grandma's memory. Somewhere high in the trees, a peregrine falcon called to its brethren. We both stopped to listen for a moment, letting Grandpa's words float downstream.

"I'm sorry Grandma's not here," I said. "I always liked her."

"Everybody liked her," Grandpa replied with a sigh.

"Yeah," I agreed. "She made the best homemade bread and marionberry jam and peanut butter cookies."

Grandpa nodded, and we grew silent again, returning our focus to the water, lost in our thoughts.

"You know your dad and I used to fish here all the time when he was young. We would come down here after school and stay until dark. I could never tell if he enjoyed it or only tolerated it, he was always so . . ."

Grandpa's voice trailed off and the melody of the creek filled the void. I watched him as he concentrated on the water, and imagined his head crowded with memories.

"I like fishing," I said as I reeled in my line, casting it back out into a small eddy downstream. "I like it out here on the river."

I didn't know why I said that or even why I liked it. Maybe the change of pace from the garden attracted me, or the relaxed rhythm of the river. It felt comfortable, like home, and it reminded me of time spent with my dad. I didn't want to complain, but I felt a bit bolder.

"Let's catch something for dinner tonight, so we don't have to eat stew."

I glanced at Grandpa as my statement hung in the air between us. To my surprise, my unexpected enthusiasm evoked the slightest twinge of a smile on the old man's face, a visible crack in his armor.

CHAPTER 15
NOW

After endless waiting, the jingle of keys moves back down the hall toward my cell. I stand up, expecting to see my lawyer. I want to get out of here. Instead, it's Olvera. "Your lawyer's here."

He frees the lock and holds the bars open for me to exit. I resist the urge to sprint past him and race down the hall away from this place. But I don't want to compound my troubles, so I step out of the cage and follow his instructions to walk down the corridor. Just before we reach the end, where a window offers a meager glimpse of daylight, he stops and points toward another passage.

"Down there. In the room on the left."

Without responding, I turn and stroll in my slippers. They make a funny *shish, shish, shish* sound as I walk. Fluorescent lighting shines from above onto the scuffed floors and naked walls. I can feel Olvera watching me closely, probably to make sure I don't ditch. I peek inside the room and see a young woman with blonde hair wearing a black business suit. When she notices me standing at the door, she approaches and extends her right arm. I reach to shake her hand.

"I'm Andrea Salvo, your attorney. Please, sit down. Are you Nash Atherton?"

Her hand feels soft, dry and cool. *She must spend her time inside reading books or doing crossword puzzles. I hope this means she remains calm under pressure.* My calloused and clammy hand exposes my working class status, and I am certain she resists the urge to wipe hers on her suit after we touch. I sit in a wooden chair near the table and study Andrea. She has a pretty face, but not in a conventional way. Her wide-set green eyes make her angular nose look slightly off-center. She can't be much older than I am.

"Are you Nash Atherton?" she asks again.

"Yes, sorry. I'm a little disoriented. My head aches. What time is it?"

"It's just after three in the afternoon. The file says they brought you in around eight this morning, so you've been here about seven hours. Have you eaten anything?"

"I had a sandwich and an apple a while ago. Can I leave now? Why are they keeping me here?" I feel restless and impatient, like I've been waiting too long for nothing to happen.

"You've been detained for questioning. They want you to talk with them or make a statement about what happened."

"I already answered their questions. What more do they want?" I ask irritably.

"You already talked to the police? Without a lawyer present?"

"Well, yeah, when they showed up at the house this morning."

"Okay, let's back up for a minute. You haven't been arrested. After twenty-four hours, you'll be free to go if they don't have enough evidence to arrest you."

I look at Andrea, and she seems too young to be a lawyer. There are no wrinkles on her face, no gray hairs on her head. "How old are you?" I ask.

"Twenty-nine."

"Oh, you look younger."

"Thank you, I guess."

"Are you a real lawyer?"

She smiles at me and her cheeks flush. "You mean, did I go to law school and pass the bar exam?"

"Yeah, all that stuff."

"Yes, I graduated from law school last year and passed the bar exam, but I also have a master's degree in social work. I worked in the child welfare office before I went to law school."

"Is that supposed to make me feel better?"

"I don't know. I'm here because I want to help people who don't have the resources to help themselves."

"You mean poor people, like me."

"Not just lower income folks, but also people who don't have contacts or know lawyers."

"Okay. I just want to get out of here."

"I'm going to do whatever I can to help you. Can you tell me what happened, why you called 911?"

I scratch my head and exhale a deep sigh. *I remember the details about what happened, but do I have to reveal them all right now? Does she need to know everything? Where should I start?*

My voice quavers when I speak. "I can trust you, right? I can tell you what happened and it's just between you and me?"

"Yes, Nash, our conversation is a privileged communication. That means it's confidential, just between you and me. Does that make sense?"

"Yeah. But what about cameras? Are we being recorded?"

"No," she says as she shakes her head and her eyes search the barren room. "There are no cameras or recording devices in here. It's just you and me talking. Nobody else will hear this."

"Okay. Does my mom know I'm here? I used my phone call to

contact your office, not her."

"Yes, I believe the police called to inform her of the situation. If you want, I can reach out to her as well."

"I think you should. She's going to be pretty upset about all this. It's probably better if you talk to her."

"Sure, I can do that."

"Thanks."

"So, what happened?"

"Well, I woke up and Grandpa was dead."

"And you called 911?"

"Yes."

"Was he still in bed when you found him?"

"No. He was sitting in his chair."

"His chair?"

"His favorite chair. No one sat in it except him."

"And how old was he?"

"Seventy-two."

"Okay, that's old, but not really old. Was he sick?"

"Yeah, he had a bad cough, chest pain, and trouble breathing. Bronchitis or asthma or something."

"Did he go to the doctor to get treatment for his illness?"

"For a while, but then he stopped."

"Hmm. I glanced at the police statement and read about their belief that you committed a crime. It said your grandfather had a recent head wound."

"Yeah."

"Do you know how he got the gash on his head?"

"It was an accident. He fell."

"All right. I think it's fine to make a statement about those things, but the report also said when you called 911 you told them you heard gunshots and a possible intruder."

"I think someone was in the house, but he left before I got up."

"What makes you think that?"

"I heard footsteps and the front door slam. I told the cops that this morning."

"You're sure about that?"

"Yes, definitely."

"Do you remember what else you told the police?"

"The basic stuff: names, living situation, you know."

"Did they ask you any other questions?"

"Maybe. It's kind of a blur. They asked me if I killed him."

"What did you say?"

"Nothing. I didn't answer."

"What? You answered some of the questions but not that one?"

"I didn't want to answer that one. Is that bad?"

"Well, it's not good, Nash. It gives the impression that you have something to hide. But it's also not bad because you didn't admit to anything."

"I was scared. They had guns and clubs and Tasers. I wanted to cooperate, but I thought I'd said enough."

"I understand. And did they read you your rights? Tell you that you had the right to remain silent?"

"Yeah, but not until after a bunch of questions. Just before they put me in the car."

"Okay. I'll review that. They might have neglected proper procedure, but since they didn't arrest you, your statements are probably admissible."

"Oh."

"But if they had probable cause to suspect you committed a crime before they began questioning, I might be able to get some of your responses omitted."

"Whatever you say."

"So you know, you can refuse to answer a police officer's questions, except when they ask you to provide your name. They just don't tell you that until they arrest or detain you."

CHAPTER 16

THEN

As June crept by with its long days and damp nights, Grandpa made sure to set aside time for fishing. He also taught me how to shoot a bow. It took a lot of strength and patience to draw the bow and release the arrow on a straight trajectory, but once I got the hang of it, I could hit the bull's-eye. He set up paper targets on the trees for me to practice. I enjoyed the challenge and the prospect of shooting a crossbow in the near future. Grandpa promised to teach me, but I needed to become more consistent with the regular bow and not lose so many arrows in the woods.

During our walks to and from the creek, Grandpa pointed out certain plants that grew near the path.

"Look over here," Grandpa said, pointing to his right.

"Where?"

"Leaves of three, let it be."

"Three leaves?"

"Yes, that plant over there. That's poison ivy, and poison oak is similar. Stay away from them if you can, and try not to touch 'em."

"I remember that from our camping trips. They're poison?"

"I don't think they can kill you, but they cause a devilish rash."

We walked a little longer and Grandpa stopped again. "See that?"

"What?"

"Over there." He pointed to his left toward the creek. "That bush with the sawtooth leaves."

"I see it."

"Stinging nettles."

For obvious reasons, you didn't want to touch those, either. Since we often wandered along the stream while fishing, I needed to know which plants to avoid when I made my way back to the house.

Grandpa also took me hunting for mushrooms one morning. In the shade and crevices of decaying logs, yellowfoot chanterelles bloomed like flowers. We gathered them to add flavor to soup or meat. In the more open areas, clusters of hearty meadow mushrooms erupted in the grass. They tasted good, but Grandpa instructed me to stay away from death cap mushrooms, the ones with white spots on them. As the name suggested, they were deadly if ingested.

I called my mom again one evening near the summer solstice to check in. She had left me a voicemail a couple days before. This time she answered my call, relieved to hear that Grandpa and I were doing well.

"You should see the huge vegetable garden we planted."

"Sounds great, Nash. I'm sure it's been a lot of hard work."

"So hard, but everything is growing, and we're fishing, too."

"Really? Have you caught anything?"

"A few small ones, but Grandpa got a huge trout the other day that was beautiful. We ate it for dinner that same night."

"Wow, fresh fish."

"And guess what? Grandpa is teaching me to shoot a bow."

"A bow with arrows?"

"Yeah, like Katniss in *The Hunger Games*. We've got targets set up on some of the trees."

"You're being careful, though, right? That sounds dangerous."

"We're careful, Mom. Don't worry. We don't aim at people."

"Okay, well, I have news for you, too."

"What's that?"

"I got promoted to a day shift at the hospital."

"That's great, Mom. You finally have a normal schedule."

"Yeah, it's really wonderful."

"Maybe you can come down and visit us on your day off. I want to show you the garden and how to shoot a bow. I can sleep in the tent."

"I'll think about it. Maybe in a few weeks. I'm pretty busy with other things right now."

"Like what?"

"I have group therapy, and I also signed up to take a yoga class."

"Sounds fun, I guess."

"It is. I like it."

"If you say so."

"And how is Grandpa? How's his cough?"

"Um, fine, I think. Do you want to talk to him?"

"If he's there, I'll talk to him."

I handed the phone over to Grandpa. He reassured her that we had lots to do, and his cough hadn't progressed. When Mom and I resumed our conversation, we didn't have much to say, but promised to connect again soon. To my surprise, she didn't mention my call and sporadic texts to Eric. I guessed she didn't actually monitor my cell usage.

I tried to work out a deal with Eric and assure him I could pay my debt to Carl. The negotiation proved troublesome, though, because the signal faded in and out. When he pressed for a face-to-face meeting, I balked. It seemed like a bad idea to lure them to Drift Creek, so I made up excuses and feigned ignorance about my exact location. I didn't want Grandpa entangled in my problem, especially since our relationship had only just improved.

In the evenings, Grandpa and I settled into a routine of listening to the radio, reading, or playing backgammon. We talked about the weather forecast, recent newspaper articles, and the garden. Other times we told each other stories: Grandpa about his time as a Marine or working as a machinist, and me about school, friends, and plans for the future. We didn't stay up late because we always woke up early for a full day of chores.

One afternoon, when our work seemed endless, Grandpa announced that he needed to make a trip to town. I stopped digging and dropped my shovel in the dirt.

"Yippee! I'm going with you."

"No, you're not!" he countered.

"What? I have to go. I can't work all the time."

"You can take a break and go fishing if you want, or read one of your books."

"No! I want to get out of here."

"I know you do, and that's exactly why you're staying."

"But that's not fair. You're treating me like a prisoner."

"You can take the afternoon off."

"That's lame. I'm going with you."

"No, you're not. You're not ready."

"That's stupid!" I yelled, spitting into the soil. "I am ready!"

"Your anger tells me you're not."

"Frickin' a, that's not fair. Haven't I been punished enough?"

"This ain't punishment. It's therapy."

"That's total crap, and you know it. I'm fine, and I'll be finer if I'm not trapped here."

But Grandpa ignored my pleas, and when he left, I threw my gloves onto the ground and stomped on them until they were covered with dirt. I stormed into the house and slammed the door, my arms bent at the elbows, fingers clenched.

"Fuck!" I screamed, then punched the wall in the kitchen. The drywall was cheap and thin, and my fist went through cleanly with little pain. After a few minutes, with ice on my hand, I calmed down and marched to Grandpa's bedroom. I had found a key in the drawer of his bedside table, and I wanted to see if it opened the secret cabinet in the kitchen.

I was in luck. The old brass key slid perfectly into the lock, and a gentle turn to the right released it. As I eased the door open, the faint odor of varnish tickled my nose. I peered inside, thinking it would be crammed with hidden treasure. Instead, the shelves were empty except for a small photo album and a bottle of Jack Daniels. Although I was interested in the pictures, the whiskey seized my attention. As I stared at the amber liquid, saliva collected under my tongue. I reached for the bottle but stopped.

No. Don't do it. Leave it alone. You don't need it. But another part of me taunted that first voice. *Yes, you wimp. Finders' keepers, take a swig. You deserve it. You earned it.*

Annoyed by my internal debate, I grabbed a glass from the sink, unscrewed the top of the bottle, and poured myself some whiskey.

CHAPTER 17
NOW

After spending twenty-four hours in the pen, I figure they're going to let me go. It turns out I'm wrong. When Andrea comes back the next day, she breaks the news.

"They're going to arrest you. They think they can prove you killed your grandfather."

"What? How's that possible?"

"I know it's not what you wanted to hear."

"So, I have to stay in jail?"

"For now, yes, until we can get you released on bail."

Olvera appears at the door of the interview room. "Nash Atherton, you're under arrest for killing Fredrick Atherton. Would you like to make a statement?"

I look at Andrea and she shakes her head.

"No," I reply.

As I shuffle into the other room with Olvera, Andrea informs me she'll be back this afternoon.

"Don't answer any questions, okay?"

"Okay."

Mug shots come next, and I look wretched, just like everyone else who has been forced in front of this camera. At least nobody expects me to smile. Then they want fingerprints, and I notice the dirt under my nails. *Why didn't I wash them in the sink in my cell?* Unsure about what to do if they inspect my extremities, I rub them on my jeans. Thankfully, Olvera doesn't notice and gives me an alcohol wipe, instructing me to clean my hands. I scrub vigorously and then try to relax as he leads me to a digital scanner connected to a computer. He presses the fingers of my left hand to the glass, and waits for a reading. After a few moments, my prints appear on the computer screen, and he presses my thumb onto the glass. Then he rolls each of my fingers before we repeat the process with my right hand.

Olvera finishes with me and transfers me to Casey, who is sitting behind a desk.

"Empty your pockets," she says.

"They are empty. They took my stuff yesterday."

"Yes, I see that in the record. One pocketknife and one cell phone, correct?"

"Yup."

"Here, change into these," she says, handing me an orange shirt and drawstring pants that are a cross between scrubs and pajamas.

"Right here?" I ask.

"Here is fine, or you can step behind the curtain over there," she says, pointing to her left.

"What should I do with my clothes?"

"Put them in here," Casey says, holding a large plastic bag open for my T-shirt and jeans. "It's time to get you back to the cell."

I look like a traffic cone in head-to-toe orange, but what do I care? I haven't worn clean clothes for weeks. Casey grasps my arm, and I glance down the hall. In less than a minute, I'm back in the dungeon, and the bars close behind me. I have nothing to do but wait and think. *My mom is really going to be mad now.*

When Andrea returns, I'm itching to get up and walk around. I'm going stir-crazy just sitting in that cell and look forward to the short stroll down the hall to the interview room. Andrea is sitting at the table, and I jump right in with a question.

"What's going on? Can I get out of here now? I hate not knowing anything."

"Slow down, Nash. It takes a while to gather evidence, but I do have the initial report from Deputy Hanson."

"What does it say?" I reply, pacing back and forth in the tiny room.

Andrea studies me before responding. "If you sit down, I'll read you the report. But you should know, it's not all the information in the case. The police are still investigating, and they may find evidence at the scene that hasn't made it into a report yet. They'll interview witnesses, like neighbors, relatives, friends, or anyone who might know something about what happened. Finally, the medical examiner will perform an autopsy and provide a detailed report of his findings. There are still a lot of unanswered questions."

"Okay, fine. I just want to know what's in the report."

CHAPTER 18
THEN

When Grandpa got home, he found me passed out on the kitchen floor, the nearly empty bottle and open photo album nearby.

"What the devil is going on here?"

I responded with a groan, then curled up into the fetal position. My head rested on the floor, only inches from the door. My stomach churned, and my temples felt like they were being squeezed in a vice. I couldn't open my eyes. Grandpa leaned over and poked me in the back with his finger.

"Are you awake? You need to get rid of that poison," he said. I moaned, and he prodded me in the back until I managed to get on my hands and knees. "Crawl toward the door. If you're going to be sick, at least keep it outside."

I dragged myself to the stoop and stuck my head out. I swayed slightly, closing my eyes, letting the fresh air hit my face and enter my lungs. Grandpa went around me down the steps, retrieved a small container from the compost bin, and brought it close to me. The sight of rotting garbage reminded me of intestines. The smell of decaying food waste made me heave.

For the next few minutes, the entire contents of my stomach spewed down the steps and into the yard. When I reached the point of exhaustion, my throat burning and my abs cramping, I crawled back inside. Grandpa gave me a towel and some water. I wiped my mouth, took a few sips, and inched my way back to the bedroom and the comfort of my cot.

When I awoke the next morning, Grandpa was already outside working. I drank more water and ate a piece of toast with butter. My head pounded, and my muscles ached, but I got dressed and stumbled out to the garden.

"Look what the cat dragged in!" Grandpa exclaimed upon seeing me.

"Yeah, I know. I'm a half-dead rodent."

"You're alive, that's something."

"Yup. Alive."

"Did you take a shower? That might help."

"No, I thought I should come out and work."

"How about we make today your day off?"

"Okay. If you say so."

"You're not fit for working."

I didn't argue with Grandpa. I showered and crawled back into bed. I slept the rest of the day and only emerged from my cave when I smelled hamburgers cooking on the grill. We sat on opposite sides of the table in the kitchen, and I devoured two patties with ketchup and mustard before speaking.

"Sorry I drank your stash."

Grandpa chewed slowly, lowering his burger onto the plate in front of him. I felt his steady gaze on me, and bowed my head, biting my lip to keep it from quivering.

"I'm disappointed, Nash, but I won't even ask what you were thinking."

I didn't respond immediately. "I thought I could just have one glass, and stop being mad about having to stay home."

"But you couldn't stop after one. You had to keep drinking."

"I liked how it felt to get buzzed and forgot that having more doesn't necessarily make it better."

"Getting drunk doesn't solve anything, but I suppose you know that."

"I know."

"What about breaking into my locked cabinet?"

"I guess I screwed that up, too."

"Did it occur to you that it was locked for a reason?"

"I just wanted to know what was in there."

"If you'd asked me, I would have told you."

"I know, but I was angry."

"So when you're angry, you break into people's private stores?"

"It's not like that. I thought I would take a peek and close it back up. You would never know."

"Hmm. But it didn't work out that way."

"No, it didn't, but at least I used the key."

"The key you stole from my bedroom."

"Oh. Yeah, sorry about that."

"And this hole in the wall?"

"Crud. Everything I did was wrong."

"Yes, that's true, but at least you're being honest about it. That's a step in the right direction."

CHAPTER 19
NOW

As I stretch my legs out under the table, I try to relax. I'm anxious to hear what's in the report, but it's hard to sit still. I shift in the chair a few times before Andrea starts reading. "On August eighteenth, at approximately 6:00 a.m., I was notified via radio by Central Dispatch of a 911 call from 3400 Drift Creek Road. I was informed that the caller was difficult to hear, possibly because of a poor phone connection, but was a juvenile male. The caller stated that someone had died, there might be an intruder, and he'd heard gunshots. I requested backup since I knew the area was isolated and heavily forested. I also requested that an ambulance be sent to the scene. I informed the other responding deputy to be on the lookout for suspicious people in the area.

"Deputy Davis and I arrived at 3400 Drift Creek Road at approximately 6:25 a.m. in light rain. The property had a long gravel driveway that led to a grassy clearing with an older single-wide mobile home. No persons were visible in the yard when we arrived. There was an old Ford pickup truck with expired Oregon plates parked in the driveway. We stopped and exited our vehicles with caution and guns at the ready, but still set on safety. I took the steps and approached the front door, knocked, announced our arrival, and verbally ordered anyone inside to open the door. Then I backed down the steps and waited with my weapon aimed at the door.

"Less than a minute later, the door opened and a teenage boy appeared. I ordered him to put his hands up in the air where we could see them and step outside. The boy complied with my commands, and I approached him and told him to stand still so we could check for weapons. Davis patted down the suspect and found a knife in his front pants pocket. Considering the blood on his shirt and the reported death, gunshots and intruder, we had probable cause to suspect he had committed a crime."

"They took my pocketknife and my cell phone," I interrupt.

Andrea looks at me. "Those items will be submitted into evidence."

"Evidence? Of what?"

"Of a crime. They'll check for blood on the knife and review your phone records."

"Oh."

"Are you worried about the knife?"

"No, the knife is clean."

"Okay, then we'll deal with the cell phone later. What's clear is they had probable cause to suspect a crime."

"So?"

"So they needed to read you your rights before asking you a bunch of questions."

Andrea looks at me then continues with the report. "I asked if anyone else was inside the house, and the boy said his grandfather was there and possibly dead, which gave us consent to enter the premises because we believed a person was in need of immediate aid. Davis entered the building to find and assist the victim.

"After approximately five minutes, Davis stepped back outside and confirmed there was no one inside, except an elderly male, and that he was dead. Davis stated that the deceased was clothed, semi-upright in a chair, and appeared to have a large wound on the side of his head that looked suspicious. I cancelled the ambulance and notified the coroner that we would need an autopsy." Andrea pauses and turns the page. "This next part is about the questioning. It says Deputy Hanson read you your rights, then he told you, the suspect, that you had the right to remain silent and not answer questions. Did he do that?"

"Not right then. He asked a lot of questions first."

"And you answered most of them?"

"Yeah, my name, that I'd called 911, what happened."

"How did you answer that last one?"

"I woke up and found Grandpa dead."

"Did you also tell them about hearing gunshots and a possible intruder?"

"Yeah. I told them all of that."

"I know we've been over this, but at what point did you stop answering questions?"

"When they asked if I killed him."

"Okay. Let's see what the report says." Andrea turned back to the pages in front of her. "Deputy Davis asked if the suspect had seen or heard any other people or an intruder. Atherton said he heard someone, but didn't see anyone. Davis asked him what he had heard. Atherton said he heard the front door slam, and footsteps outside on the gravel. He was unclear about whether he heard the gunshots before or after hearing the door and the footsteps. Because of this uncertainty, my experience tells me he is lying or withholding information about what happened. I then asked him if he killed his grandfather. Atherton refused to answer that question and stated he would not answer any more questions. He did not deny killing his grandfather.

"I then informed the suspect he was being detained for questioning. I handcuffed him to prevent him from fleeing and led him to my patrol car. When he was secure in the back seat, I drove to the station."

Andrea looked up again. "I will make an argument that your answers are inadmissible because you weren't informed of your right to remain silent before he started asking you anything, but it's a stretch. You hadn't been arrested or detained at that point."

"But I felt like I was detained. Like I didn't have the option to leave."

"I'll make that argument and see if it sticks. If not, we'll address the timing of everything, when he read you your rights. That might be your word against his, depending on what Deputy Davis's report says."

"He didn't tell me about my rights until he handcuffed me."

"Okay, we'll wait and see. At this point, the most damaging thing in the report is that you didn't deny killing your grandfather. After answering all the other questions, you raised suspicions by not denying it."

"Oh."

"That's okay. We can work with it. It may not be so damaging if we can get the earlier stuff omitted. Otherwise, we just have to see what turns up during the investigation."

"So, it's going to take a while?"

"Yes, very few things happen quickly in court."

"Do I have to stay here or can somebody bail me out?"

"For now, you have to stay. We won't know about bail until we get you in front of a judge."

"Will that be tomorrow?"

"Tomorrow or Tuesday. I'll let you know as soon as I can."

"So, I just wait?"

"That's about all you can do."

Several loud thumps shake the door, and Olvera bursts into the room, interrupting my thoughts. He sees me sitting at the table, but addresses Andrea. "Ms. Salvo, I've got orders to move the suspect to a cell at the courthouse."

"Right now?"

"Yes. I'm off-duty in less than an hour, and I have orders to take him over before I finish for the day. He'll wait there for arraignment."

"Okay, thank you."

"You can meet your client over there if you want, but this meeting is over."

"All right, but just one more minute, please. I have a final question for Nash."

Olvera glares at me and scowls, but agrees. "I'll step outside, but only for a minute."

When the door closes behind him, Andrea turns and sits down at the table across from me. She leans in close, and I can smell her perfume and see the faint outline of a blemish forming on her cheek. She doesn't speak right away, but looks at me the way my mom does when she knows there is more to the story, like she wants to help but doesn't quite know how to get through to me. I think she's going to ask me if I killed my grandpa, but I'm wrong.

"Get some rest Nash. I'll see you tomorrow. I should have the other report by then, and we can talk about options for bail, and how you want to plead."

Before I can respond, she stands, gathers the file along with her notepad and briefcase, and heads for the door. After opening it, she pauses like she has one final question. Instead, she gives me a weak smile.

"You'll be okay. See you tomorrow."

CHAPTER 20
THEN

W
e remained quiet for the rest of the meal. I ate a third burger then stood to collect the dirty plates. I was shocked Grandpa hadn't yelled at me or kicked me out. "Are you going to tell my mom about all this?" I asked.

"No, I think we can keep this between us. But if it happens again, I'll have to tell her."

"It won't happen again, I promise."

"All right then. Let's get these dishes cleaned."

We buried the topic, and by the end of June, took regular breaks from the garden to go fishing. We enjoyed the challenge of catching our next meal, and the clear, crisp, running water eased our discomfort and drew us closer. While we waded in the creek and tossed our hooks into the shady grottos, Grandpa told me about Grandma Helen, how they met, and their life together. I learned that Grandma loved poetry and jigsaw puzzles, and was an only child like me. She baked cookies every week and would read to the garden gnomes when she was lonely. I couldn't resist adding to the stories.

"One of the best things about our camping trips here was at night, when Grandma brought hot chocolate with marshmallows out to our tent. She always gave me extra marshmallows."

"Oh, I remember that. Even on warm evenings she wanted to bring you cocoa."

"And she let me use her binoculars to explore. I made sure to use the strap and wear them around my neck so I wouldn't drop them."

"She said you were very careful. That's why she let you use them."

"Grandma let me use her Swiss Army knife, too. I felt like a pioneer whittling arrows, hunting bears, and eating the kill. I had an imagination back then."

"You sure did, and I've still got that knife. I should pass it along to you."

"Thanks, Grandpa."

"I'm sorry we didn't continue the camping after she died. I just couldn't function without her. I still miss her every day."

I remained silent for a while, remembering the little things that made Grandma special.

"I know what you mean. When someone you love disappears, if feels like nothing will ever fill that void."

We didn't mention it again until one afternoon, when we worked our way upriver in search of trout. Grandpa asked if I wanted to talk about Jeff, his son and my dad. He'd posed a risky question, given our prior history with the subject, and I detected the restraint in his voice. He was reluctant to broach a topic that might set me off in an unknown direction. I tried to avoid thinking about my dad, so I paused before answering.

"Most of the time it doesn't seem like he's dead," I said. "I still think of him as living in Alaska."

I avoided the reality that I'd never see or talk to my dad again by pretending he lived somewhere else. It was easier that way. After he left, but before he died, Mom always told me not to get my hopes up or waste time thinking about him. But I couldn't stop wondering why he left, or hoping he'd come back. *How could someone walk away from their own son?* I promised myself, if I ever became a father, I would never do that to my child.

"Do you think about him?" I tentatively asked Grandpa.

"Yes," he replied without hesitation. "It broke your grandma's heart when he left. She was devastated. He said goodbye over the phone, and she stayed in bed for days. When she finally got up, I think she recognized that life continued, even if you didn't want it to. I'm relieved she went to heaven hoping and believing that Jeff would return to his family."

He paused and looked downstream, either to hide his grief or search for a sign that Grandma rested peacefully. When he resumed, his voice dropped an octave.

"Sometimes I think it's my fault. That he left because of me, that I was too hard on him."

"Why were you hard on him?" I asked, unable to stop myself.

Grandpa waited to respond, fiddling with his fishing line and wading farther into the stream, away from me.

"It was a long time ago. When Jeff was just a boy." Grandpa paused again, seemingly hypnotized by the rushing water that surrounded us. I remained still, not sure if I should say anything, and Grandpa continued. "I was hard on him all his life. Maybe I expected too much from him. And I got mad at him so many times for so many reasons. That was his whiskey in the cabinet. The last time he was here, I took it away from him. He had a problem with alcohol, and I've had the bottle locked away ever since."

Grandpa surrendered a sigh filled with pain and regret. He struggled in that moment and grasped his shirt near the collar. He pressed it to his chest and bowed his head, visibly anguished. I watched him closely but kept my distance. Before long, Grandpa spoke again.

"I wasn't surprised that he left, but I hoped he'd stay in touch with you. It's so easy these days with your little phone gadgets. I also hoped he would quit drinking and be able to keep a job. I never thought he'd take his own life."

It sounded like Grandpa had stopped being angry with his son, but the finality of the situation crushed him. He felt powerless to do anything but embrace his sorrow. Even after talking with the therapist, Larry, I didn't know how I felt about my dad. Angry? Disappointed? Sad? Confused? Most of the time, it was all of the above. But now I realized I had Grandpa to help me through the tough times.

CHAPTER 21
NOW

E ven though I have no plans to escape, Olvera handcuffs me for the move to the courthouse. It's a short drive in the back of a squad car, and I feel depressed. I had hoped to go home today. Instead, they're moving me to a different jail. I hope it's quiet like the old one. I don't want to hear other people talking trash, and I don't want anyone bothering me.

No such luck. I soon discover the courthouse jail is bright, loud and chaotic. Inmates howl at each other and at me as Olvera walks me through. They bang on the bars, whistle, and shout obscenities. The guards strut around, patrolling the area with shifty eyes and frowning faces. Thankfully, we clear the zoo and disappear around a corner.

"Juveniles don't hafta stay out there with the animals," says Olvera with a smirk. "You get a little privacy."

I nod my head. *Thank god I don't have to be out there with the wolves.*

My new cell is smaller, darker, and feels more confining than the last. A thin mattress is rolled tightly on the bunk, and a pillow and blanket peek out from the side. I unroll the cylinder and arrange my bed. A musty odor hits my nose, and the flattened pillow reminds me of a discarded stuffed animal. *How many heads have rested on this lump of foam? Were any of them able to sleep?*

Sitting there alone, I have nothing to do but think. I could be charged with a serious crime, but I won't know that until tomorrow or the next day. The guard brings me dinner, but I'm not hungry. I push the food around the tray, wondering what will happen tomorrow. *What did Andrea say? Depending on what the investigators find, they could charge me with murder, and try me as an adult?* That sick feeling gnaws at my gut again, twisting and writhing like a fish caught on a hook. I stand and pace back and forth, comforted by the *shish, shish, shish* sound of my slippers.

Andrea seems smart and perceptive. Despite my nerves and anxiety, she made me feel at ease. *I really hope she can get me out of here. Her questions were good, but should I have told her everything that happened?* She might not like what I have to say. *I disclosed the most important parts, and everything I said was true.* I just couldn't bring myself to say more. *Can I really trust her?* I don't have much of a choice.

I wish she had left me a copy of the report, though. I want to go over the part about hearing an intruder and gunshots. I know what I heard, but I'm not certain what I told the police. The details from that morning are fuzzy, and I need to replay the events in my mind. I have to remember exactly what I heard, what I saw, and what I did before calling 911.

CHAPTER 22
THEN

One July morning, as I feasted on fried eggs and toast, Grandpa showed up late to the breakfast table. It seemed strange for him to lag at this hour. When he appeared, he handed me a written list of chores for the day.

"What's this?" I asked between bites. "Why do I need a list?"

"I'm making a trip to town for supplies and things. You're staying here to hold down the fort."

"What?" I said, leaping at the opportunity. "I want to go with you this time!"

"Not today, Nash. I need you here working."

"But that's not fair. You know it. I've been here for months doing nothing but work. I need a break, too!"

"Not today," he grumbled, grabbing the keys to the truck and stuffing his wallet and a white business card into his pocket. The tone of his voice told me he wouldn't change his mind, so I sat back down to finish breakfast.

I remembered when he drove to town a few weeks before. I had pitched a fit about going along, then proceeded to spend my day getting into all kinds of trouble. There wasn't any liquor in the house this time, but Grandpa never considered that I might find other ways to occupy my time. A caged animal always looks for a way out, and I had found one once. Not a full-blown escape, but a way to connect with the outside world and my friend.

Grandpa fumbled with some things on the counter while I quietly fumed. It seemed pointless to beg. Grandpa had made his decision. I was stuck at home.

Before leaving, Grandpa broke the silence. "We can go into town next week, but not today."

"Okay," I replied dully, trying not to care as he headed toward the door. Even though I had been a brat about staying home last time, Grandpa brought me some cheap arrows for target practice. I appreciated the gesture, but I longed for a little freedom in town, a giant slice of pizza, and a chance to talk to Eric.

As Grandpa got ready to leave, the old telephone on the counter sprang to life with an annoying jangle. It startled me, because I had never heard it ring. We used it to call my mom, but nobody ever called here. Grandpa answered it with a rough greeting, and then frowned as he listened. I only heard his side of the conversation, if you could call it that.

"Yes. Yes. I'll be there." Then he hung up without saying goodbye.

I watched Grandpa, waiting for him to give me some indication about who called, but he kept his back to me, fidgeting with the buttons on his shirt.

"Who was that?" I ventured, not expecting an answer but definitely curious.

"None of your business," said Grandpa as he opened the door to leave. "I'll be back before sunset. You best get to work before it rains."

After the door closed, I heard the gritty whine of the truck engine, and the crunch of gravel beneath the tires. As Grandpa pulled away, a small cloud of dust hung in the air like an ancient smoke signal, then disappeared.

I let out a frustrated screech. How could he do that to me? I wanted to throw my plate across the room and watch it shatter into a thousand pieces. I had worked so hard, done everything Grandpa told me, and deserved a chance to go to town. The longer I thought about it, the more pissed off I got.

I had been there longer than two months and never once left the property, at least by driving. I couldn't be sure about the size of Grandpa's land or the property lines because fences didn't crisscross the forest. I wandered for almost an hour near the creek the last time he left me alone. I embarked on an adventure of sorts, but not like a kid pretending to track wild animals. My mission had been to locate a strong cell signal, and I'd succeeded. I knew I'd go hunting again today.

After hastily completing the essential chores, I grabbed my crummy little phone and threw a windbreaker and some fishing gear into my backpack. I marched toward the creek, using the worn trail at the far corner of the yard. Dense clouds loomed above, and the wind unsettled the tops of the trees, sending them waving in all directions. I ignored the low rumble of thunder in the distance.

When I got to Drift Creek, I baited my hook even though I felt too agitated to fish. I couldn't relax, be patient, and follow the rhythm of the river. My frustration with Grandpa distracted me, so I abandoned my gear near a large boulder and took off walking.

As I hiked, it started to drizzle, and the wind gusted from the west. I put on my jacket and stepped around giant ferns and fallen trees, trying to envision my previous route. After at least thirty minutes, I descended into a gully that collected water, and climbed a steep slope up the other side. I couldn't remember where I'd explored before, and I didn't want to get lost. *Why hadn't I marked some trees as a guide?*

That would've been the smart thing to do. The area didn't look familiar, and the dense leafy plants surrounding me obstructed my view.

Ping! The bell-like tone indicated I had a message on my phone. I found cell service! I seized the device and saw a text from an unknown number. I protected the screen from the rain and opened the message.

> *This is E. New number. Delete old one. Contact me right away.*

I couldn't tell when he sent me the message. It could have been days or even weeks ago. Eric and I talked the last time I ventured out here, but on his old number. Why did he get a new one? It seemed suspicious, but not exactly out of the ordinary considering I had a different cell number, too. I had sent him a similar text in May, explaining my circumstances, the isolation, and lack of communication. He had replied instantly.

What a relief it had been to reconnect with my old friend. He told me he attended summer school, worked every day, and earned good money. I wanted more contact with my friend, and my chance had arrived. After briefly hesitating, I texted the new number as he'd requested. I didn't wait long for a response.

> *Hey N. What took so long? You home?*

I typed back.

> *Not home. Still in the boonies. No cell service.*
> *Damn. Long sentence. What's closest town?*

I paused a moment to think before replying.

Waldport, I think. Haven't been there yet. Maybe next week.

For a few minutes after I hit send, my cell remained silent. As I waited, the patter of rain drops on my jacket and the surrounding plants absorbed my attention. The tiny drumbeats blocked out all other sounds until my phone sprang to life again.

Next Friday. Be outside IGA at noon.
Waldport? Will try. Might not work.
Waldport. Better work. Carl wants his money. Done waiting.

I typed furiously.

What? I don't have it. Not making money this summer.
Get the money or else.
C'mon E. U know I'm good for it. Just don't have it now. Need it now.
Can't we work something out?
If yur not there next Fri, we'll get it from your ma.
NO! Don't drag her into this! I didn't rat him out.
Doesn't matter. No free rides. Somebody's gotta pay.
That's harsh.
U got a week. Get the money.

As I stood there staring in disbelief at the phone, oblivious to my surroundings, a low, gravelly voice emerged behind me.

"What're ya doing out here?"

I jumped and turned to see a bearded man wearing blue jean overalls, holding a shotgun. He stared at me as I cradled the phone in my hand.

"What're ya doing on my land? Not taking pictures, are ya?"

As I stared at the gun barrel, I slid the phone into my jacket pocket.

"No photos. I didn't take any. I was trying to get a cell signal and got lost."

"Which way'd ya come from?"

I pointed to my left, trying not to shake. "That way, other side of the ravine."

At that moment, my eyes suddenly focused on where I stood. Although I'd only seen pictures of similar scenes, I knew that hundreds of burgeoning marijuana plants surrounded me. Holy crap! I needed to get out of there right away. I had trespassed onto dangerous ground.

"Ya leaving right now!" growled the man as he swung the gun around toward me.

"I'm going!" I yelped and took off down the slope, sliding into the gully, soaking my shoes as I hit the bottom. I didn't turn back or look around, but kept my feet moving, hoping the guy wouldn't shoot me. I splashed to the other side and scurried up the slippery hillside, back to the safety of the forest.

"DON'T COME BACK!" he yelled as my footsteps crashed through the underbrush and I raced toward the creek, out of his sight. My legs ached and my lungs burned, but I kept running. After about fifteen minutes, I stopped and doubled over. When I caught my breath, I looked around and spied the creek to my right. I would follow it at a slower pace, relieved to hear its familiar babble.

CHAPTER 23
NOW

I have trouble falling asleep in the new cell. Strange noises fill the corridor, and hundreds of thoughts about Grandpa and the police scamper through my brain. I don't know when exhaustion took over, but I doubt I got more than an hour or two of sleep. I wake up early for a breakfast of runny eggs, cold bacon, and dry toast. Then they take me down a different hall to the shower.

Around 11:00, a guard leads me to a stark interview room. Andrea wears a sweatshirt and blue jeans. Her casual attire tells me we won't see a judge today. She confirms my hunch, and without wasting time on small talk, gets down to business.

"When our meeting ended yesterday, Nash, we were waiting for more information. I have some of it, but I'm pretty sure it's not the evidence they think will prove your guilt."

Andrea pauses, letting her words fill the tiny room.

"What is it?"

"The first item is Deputy Davis's report. It differs from Hanson's with respect to the recitation of your Miranda rights, specifically your right to remain silent. Davis mentions it near the end, just before they handcuff you and put you in the patrol car."

"That's when they told me that stuff, near the end."

"So that could work in your favor. It's a pivotal difference, but only if a judge agrees that they had already detained you. It's going to be tricky because Hanson will say he was just talking to you, and you replied voluntarily. You say you felt trapped, or confined, like you couldn't go anywhere."

"That's right. I was afraid to move."

"Neither officer was wearing a body camera, but both of their dash cams were running. I'm not sure those pick up conversations, but they might show the interaction between you and Hanson, including any body language that might give the impression that you felt intimidated."

"There won't be any action on the film. We just stood there waiting."

"I'll take a look anyway, just to be sure."

"Okay."

"Don't worry too much about that. From what I've read, you didn't incriminate yourself. Let's see what else is in Davis's report." Andrea shuffled the papers in front of her. "I entered the residence to locate the victim. I proceeded through the door and into the kitchen. No one was in the kitchen, so I continued to the living area and saw an elderly male in a chair. I hurried to him and attempted to find a pulse. He had none and upon touching his neck, I determined that the body was cold. The deceased's eyes were closed. He was dressed in a long sleeve shirt and long pants, with socks but no shoes. There was a wound with dried blood showed on the right side of his head, above the temple, and there were bruises on his head as well. It wasn't immediately clear what caused the injury. There was no visible evidence of an altercation, fight or robbery." Andrea pauses. "Nash, you said your grandpa fell, so there wouldn't be evidence of a fight, correct?"

"Right. We argued, but didn't fight."

"But you argued? About what?"

"Um. I don't really remember. Nothing important, just stupid stuff."

"Okay. At this point, it doesn't matter so much, but I'm sure the detectives will turn the place upside down looking for a weapon or something."

"They won't find one."

"Good, that helps. Let's see what else Davis says." Andrea turns back to the report. "I quickly searched the remainder of the home, which consisted of two small bedrooms and one bathroom. I considered the premises to be a homicide scene, and proceeded to look for other victims or the killer. No other persons were present, so I returned outside and reported one deceased male inside. I told Deputy Hanson that the death was suspicious because of the victim's head wound. We agreed to detain Atherton for questioning as a suspect. Hanson informed him of his Miranda rights and drove him to the station. I remained behind to secure the scene." Andrea looks up. "That's the first part of the report. The second part is after Davis returns with a warrant to search the premises.

"I obtained a search warrant for the premises, including inside the home, outside in the yard, and in a shed. A copy of the warrant is attached and states that were looking for any weapons, specifically ones that might match the victim's head wound, items or locations with blood or fingerprint evidence, personal articles belonging to the deceased, and any evidence of additional persons at the scene.

"I took photos of the body, and the team searched for evidence of dried blood on the floor and chair, as well as in the bathroom and kitchen. A drinking glass was found near the deceased, and we preserved it and its clear liquid contents for fingerprinting and testing. No towels, tissues or clothing with obvious blood stains were located. A crossbow and a dozen arrows were found in a cabinet near the front door, but there was no indication that the weapon had been fired inside the home. We also collected a number of tools from the kitchen, including a hammer, a twelve-inch flat metal file, and a cast iron skillet." Andrea looks up at me. "When did your grandfather fall?"

"The night before he died."

"Do you remember what time?"

"It was after dinner, so maybe around seven?"

"Did you help your grandfather after he fell?"

"Yes, I helped him up."

"What about first aid?"

"What do you mean?"

"Did you get him some tissues, a towel, a bandage?"

"Yes. He was bleeding a lot."

"Head wounds do that, lots of blood. So why didn't they find any towels or tissues or something with blood on it?"

"They noticed it on my shirt."

"Who did?"

"The tall guy with the beard, Hanson."

"I must have missed that." Andrea flips back to the other report. "Oh, here it is. He mentions the blood on your shirt, which, along with the emergency call's details, was probable cause to search you."

"He asked me about the blood on my shirt."

"What did you say? That's not in the report."

"I think I said I wouldn't answer that question."

"Okay, hmm. Did you use your shirt to stop the bleeding?"

"No."

"Then what did you use?"

"Towels from the bathroom."

"So what happened to those towels?"

"I, um, got rid of them."

"You got rid of them? How?"

"I buried them in the garden."

"Why in the world would you do that?"

"I panicked. Grandpa was dead, and the towels looked so grue-some. I felt like I had to get rid of them."

"Well let's hope they don't find them."

"Yeah, let's hope."

Andrea stares at me for a moment, then returns her focus to the paper. "Okay, let's keep reading and get to the end of the report.

"After a thorough search of the interior, which included con-fiscation of the items in the trash, I searched the exterior because Atherton claimed he heard a gunshot, footsteps, and the front door slamming. The front door looked intact, with no evidence of forced entry or a broken lock. We retrieved several fingerprints from the doorknob, which will be sent in for analysis. When we searched the exterior entry landing and steps, the rain had increased, so everything was wet. The visible footprints in the gravel driveway appeared to be from the sheriff and coroner's office personnel.

"We looked for other footprints around the outside perimeter of the house, but none were visible. There was also no immediate evidence of damage to the home's windows or siding. The truck looked like it hadn't moved in a while, as no tire tracks were evident, and the hood of the vehicle was cold. We searched the shed and found several shovels that will be tested for fingerprints and blood.

"That concerns me," says Andrea.

"What?"

"The shovels. You just told me you buried the towels. Did you use a shovel?"

"Yeah. My prints will be on the shovel. I didn't wear gloves."

"Hmm. Okay, the fingerprints are easy to explain, but we'll have to wait and see if they find any blood on the shovel."

"Oh."

"That morning, did you hear a car?"

"No, we just had the truck."

"What about voices?"

"No."

"But you heard footsteps?"

"Yup."

"You're sure?"

"I know someone was there."

"Okay. We might learn something from the front door prints, but not much else. The report concludes with Davis looking for any witnesses in the neighborhood."

"Did he talk to anyone? We don't really have close neighbors."

"I'll check on that, and see who he talked to."

"What happens now?"

"It will be several days or a week before we have the coroner's report showing the cause of death. That detail will be critical, as will any information on the blood and fingerprints."

She looks at her watch, and suddenly I'm restless. I bounce my leg and try not to fidget, but I don't know what to say or do next. Andrea seems unaware of my agitation and continues.

"The arraignment is tomorrow morning at 10:00. From my perspective, based on what's in the file, the DA doesn't have enough evidence to charge you with a crime. They will do their best to keep you here, though, since the police went to the trouble of arresting you. But the evidence looks weak."

This seems like good news—a ray of hope that I'll get out of here.

"By the way, I spoke to your mom. She plans to attend the hearing."

I look at Andrea, relieved by the news, but apprehensive at the same time. My mom might have to take time off work to be here. I want to see her, but worry it might be a wasted effort.

"Is she doing okay?"

"She's upset about your arrest and your grandfather's death, but she's okay. And she knows it's important to be here. I think she'll be helpful."

Silence fills the room as I retreat into my head with a jumble of thoughts about my mom. *When did I see her last? How angry will she be? She knew Grandpa fell, but how much did she know about his illness? Does she have money for bail? Will she help me out?*

After a few moments, Andrea pushes back her chair and stands. "There's not much more you can help with today. I've got some motions to file and telephone calls to make, but I'll be back here an hour before the hearing tomorrow."

I stare at her with a blank look. *She's going to leave me all alone in this hellhole.*

"What should I do while I'm waiting?"

"Hope they don't uncover any incriminating evidence during the next twenty-one hours."

CHAPTER 24
THEN

What a rotten day. I neglected my chores and failed to catch any fish. A crazy pot grower nearly shot me, and my best friend Eric gave me an ultimatum. I couldn't believe what he said! Bring the money or they would get it from my mom. It felt wrong to get her involved in my problem. She might think I still used drugs, and she'd probably want me to go to the police and tell them everything I knew about Carl. But that would only make things worse. She had enough troubles of her own with rehab, keeping her job, and paying bills. I didn't want her worried about me, too. But somehow, I needed to get fifteen hundred dollars in one week.

A few months ago, if faced with a dilemma like that, I would've turned to drugs and probably sold them to make the money. Or, I would've continued stealing and getting high in a lame effort to avoid the problem. Only after getting clean did I understand the twisted logic of it all.

When Grandpa returned from town, he looked older than his seventy-two years. He plopped down to rest without even saying hello. Still shaken by my encounter with the man in the woods and the toxic texts, I didn't bother asking him about his day. I put the groceries away and let him relax in his favorite chair. He dozed more frequently in the evenings, so I let him be.

As he slept, I rushed back down to the creek to retrieve my fishing gear. I left it behind in my haste to get home after the scare with the farmer. Thankfully, summer brought lengthy days, and I had no trouble finding my stuff in the twilight.

Grandpa was still rooted in his chair when I returned to the house. He didn't ask where I'd been.

"What sounds good for dinner?" I asked, as I tidied up the kitchen.

"Anything you want to make is fine," he replied, his face buried in the newspaper.

"Okay. I can make a salad. There's plenty of fresh produce."

"Salad is good."

"I might make spaghetti, too. I saw you bought some sauce."

"Fine with me."

When the meal was ready, we ate in silence, both lost in our thoughts. Grandpa didn't complain about the simple meal, and I wasn't that hungry. I had more pressing problems.

As I washed the dishes, Grandpa retired to the comfort of his worn, corduroy perch. When the kitchen looked clean, I pulled up a side chair and set up the backgammon board on a table between us. I didn't necessarily want to play, but I needed to chat with Grandpa. It seemed like the conversation flowed smoother when we occupied our hands with another task. I had no idea how or where to begin, so I asked an open-ended question, one that I hoped would get him talking and provide an opportunity find out more about his neighbor.

"What was it like being a soldier in Vietnam?"

Grandpa didn't look up as he contemplated my query and executed his opening moves after rolling double fours. When he raised his eyes, they looked glassy and wet, like the mere mention of the war brought out some long-buried emotions. He spoke in a barely audible voice.

"It was hell on earth. Every day was filled with frustration, fear, grief, doubt and regret."

His words penetrated my skull. I hadn't expected a response like that. My mouth went dry, and my armpits dampened. I cleared my throat softly and stuttered, "I-I'm sorry. I didn't mean to . . ."

But Grandpa somberly shook his head and forced himself to continue. "I don't wish that experience on anyone, even my sworn enemy. Being halfway around the world, killing strangers in their own country. Watching your buddies get ripped apart by bullets and grenades. Never sleeping because you're afraid of an ambush. Surviving each day, but wondering if it will be your last. I still have nightmares about it." He stopped speaking, bowed his head, and dabbed his eyes with his sleeve. "Why do you ask? Are you thinking of enlisting?"

"Heck no. I was out walking in the woods today and got lost. I ended up in a place I wasn't supposed to be, on the other side of a ravine. A tall, bearded guy threatened me with a gun. I was scared, so I ran off. I wondered if that was what it was like in Vietnam."

I don't know how I came up with that story, but it was at least somewhat true and explained why I would pose the question.

"So you met my neighbor, Earl Fiske," replied Grandpa with a smirk. "He's a piece of work, has lived around here longer than me. We hunt together several times a year and share the meat, but I haven't seen or heard from him in months. I thought maybe he was dead."

"Oh, he's very much alive," I said. "And he was mad as hell that I was trespassing."

"Really? That's strange. He was never the type to get too upset about that sort of thing. I wonder what got into him? You think he's getting senile?"

"I'm not sure," I said, rolling a pitiful two and one with the dice. "But I think it had something to do with his farming."

"Earl is farming? That's the craziest thing I've heard. He's older than me. He used to plant a garden like ours and raise a few cows, but farming?"

"Yeah. I hate to be the one to tell you, but it looks like your neighbor is growing marijuana. Lots of it."

"Well, I'll be dipped in doggy doo. He's growing weed?" Grandpa chuckled. "I wouldn't have figured him for that business, but if you saw it, I believe you."

"I saw it alright. Hundreds of plants that were taller than me. It was raining, and I had stopped to get my bearings. The next thing I knew, he was in front of me with a shotgun, telling me to leave."

Grandpa pondered this for a moment and took his turn with the dice. "It's good you left. You did the right thing. No point sticking around to see what he'd do. He might be paranoid about strangers snooping around, or the cops, but it's entirely possible he's got a legal operation."

"Really? Growing marijuana like that is legal?"

"Yes, if you file the right papers and follow the rules. I don't know if he's done that, but I'll call him tomorrow. At least let him know you're not a threat. You're a neighbor and it was an innocent mistake."

"Is that a good idea? It might be better to forget about it. I don't want to stir up any trouble."

"It's no trouble. Earl and I've been friends a long time. It'll be good to check in with him anyway. We old folks have to look out for each other."

"He seemed perfectly capable of looking out for himself, and it worries me that you might piss him off."

"Don't worry, Nash. It's easy to look tough when you're holding a gun. I'll call to say hello and tell him my grandson's been here for the summer. I won't inquire about his 'farming,'" he said, raising his fingers to make air quotes.

We finished the first game, and I got skunked. I hated losing, but I had no luck with the dice. As I set up the board for the next one, Grandpa declined. He said he felt too tired and wanted to go to bed early.

"What? It's never one and done. You have to play another game, so I have a chance to even up the match."

"Okay, I guess I can play one more. Could you get us some ice cream first, though?"

I sprang from my chair and sprinted to the kitchen at the mention of ice cream. We never had treats like that. When I opened the freezer, directly in front, I saw the beautiful quart of caramel butter pecan. It felt like Christmas morning.

CHAPTER 25
NOW

Alone in my cell, time passes like a snail creeping across the sidewalk. I eat lunch, then dinner, but have nothing else to do while I wait to get in front of the judge. For at least an hour, I watch the second hand on the clock sweep around and tick off each minute. I see how long I can hold my breath. I practice reciting the alphabet backward. I listen to the faint chatter of the other inmates, but it depresses me. Some of them actually sound cheerful and upbeat. *Really? How can you be happy in jail?* I try to keep my spirits up, but know it's going to be a long sleepless night.

At nine the next morning, exactly when Andrea said she'd be back, the guard leads me down the hallway to the sterile interview room. My lawyer stands with her briefcase in one hand and a new file folder in the other. She wears a dark blue suit with gold buttons on the front, and has her hair pulled back into a neat bun. Her lips are pressed together in a flat line, making the corners of her mouth droop. A slight vertical crease appears between her eyebrows.

After saying hello, she motions for me to have a seat.

"I have some additional information in your case. I'm actually surprised they revealed this before the hearing. Most DAs would keep it to themselves."

This doesn't sound good, so I shut my mouth and sit down.

"I have a copy of an arrest report from Portland, dated April sixth of this year."

Rats! They pulled the old report. I'd hoped it would stay hidden, at least for a day or two, but here it is. People get the wrong idea when they find out you have a record. They want to label you a criminal and assume you're guilty.

"Why do they have that report?" I ask defensively.

"I imagine they included it because it might be evidence of a probation violation. They can keep you in jail until your hearing if you've committed a crime while on probation. Or, the prosecutor wants to ask the judge to set your bail higher, or ask that you be held without bail."

"Geez," I say, turning away to look at the blank wall. "That sounds bad."

"It's neither good nor bad. It's just information. And the more of it we have, the better off we'll be."

I look up at Andrea. She remains calm and sounds like the voice of reason in all of this.

"Since you know what happened in April, I assume you'd like to hear about some of the other information."

I bite my lip, nod my head, and shift back in the chair to listen. Andrea sits down across from me and begins reading.

"The police have looked at the fingerprint evidence at the scene, as well as a few items found in the house."

"Okay," I say, my heart accelerating.

Andrea's tone suggests lousy news. She opens the folder and withdraws a few sheets of paper. "This is a report on the finger-prints found on the glass next to your grandfather. No surprise here. The prints match both you and the deceased. Same for the prints found on the front doorknob."

I keep my focus on Andrea as she reads. When she pauses to look at me, I'm not sure whether I'm supposed to comment. Before I can even think of a question, she resumes.

"The fingerprint report, as far as I'm concerned, isn't damaging because it only shows that you and your grandfather both touched the glass and the doorknob. It's pretty easy to explain since you lived in the same house, and maybe you brought your grandfather something to drink. The issue with the prints, which I'm sure the prosecutor will consider, is the lack of other prints in either tested location, particularly the doorknob." Andrea looks at me like a teacher who wants to make sure the whole class understands before she proceeds. "Your statement to the police mentions a possible intruder. By not finding any fingerprints from a third party, it could be presented as circumstantial evidence that no one else entered the home."

I remain quiet, absorbing the information, trying to make sense of the logic that an absence of evidence could actually be evidence. Andrea senses I am perplexed by that knowledge and offers an explanation.

"Don't worry, the absence of other fingerprints doesn't prove no one else was inside the house. It suggests that possibility, but it is not definitive proof. You and I both know it's possible to enter a home and not leave any prints. The simplest way to do that is to wear gloves."

When she mentions gloves, my heart skips a beat. My eyes dart to her face and quickly return to the table in front of me. *Did she mention gloves as a random example, or am I about to hear some unfavorable news?* She shuffles the papers and looks at me again, raising her eyebrows and silently asking if I'm ready for her to continue.

"This report is a notice of evidence taken from the scene that will be submitted for additional testing. As I mentioned, they took the glass, and now that the fingerprint evidence is complete, they will send its contents, the clear liquid, to the lab for identification."

"The glass had water in it," I blurt out. "That's what they'll find."

Andrea studies me for a moment. "Are you sure about that? Because if that's the case, then it's good news."

"I'm sure. I got Grandpa a glass of water before I went to bed."

"It will be helpful if that's what the lab results reveal. That's an easy one to explain, but there is something that will be a little more challenging. They found some THC 'candy' wrappers in one of the bedrooms. Do you know what those are, Nash?"

"Candy? You mean edibles?"

"Yes."

"They aren't mine. I'm clean. You can test my urine."

Andrea hesitates, blinking her eyes a few times and leaning back in her chair. "Let me consider that strategy. If you agree to take a drug test and are in fact clean, that could help your case. But, if the test comes back positive for THC or any substance, then it'd be better if you hadn't taken it."

"I swear I'm clean. I haven't had anything since April." *That's almost true. I got drunk on Grandpa's whiskey, but that was two months ago and nobody needs to know about that.*

"Let's see how some other things shake out first, but we'll keep that option open if we need it. As you probably know, use or consumption of marijuana by adults is legal in Oregon. And, according to the report, they were found in what appears to be your grandfather's bedroom. I'm sure the coroner will send samples of his blood to the lab for analysis."

I can't believe Grandpa had edibles. I'm glad I didn't know, because I might have been tempted to steal them. And he must have had a darn good hiding place. I turned the house upside down and found nothing.

Andrea shuffles the papers once more. "Here's a different report on some of the items found in the kitchen trash. The first is an empty prescription bottle in your grandfather's name for Restoril."

"What?" I say. "What's that?"

"It's a drug used to treat anxiety and insomnia."

"I never saw Grandpa take any pills."

"I'm guessing they will dust the bottle for fingerprints, so it will be a victory for us if it comes back with only your grandfather's prints. We'll address it later if the results are unfavorable, but the next item might be a concern. They found poisonous mushrooms in the trash: *Amanita phalloides*. The medical examiner will determine during the autopsy whether your grandfather ingested them."

"That's weird. I gathered mushrooms last week, but not the poisonous ones."

"So you've collected them before?"

"Yeah, the good kind, though: chanterelles and meadow mushrooms. Grandpa showed me the deadly ones, so I know the difference."

"Okay, we'll deal with that later also, depending on the autopsy report. But let's talk about the items found in the bathroom. They might require more explanation."

My brain whirs to life as I visualize the tiny bathroom. Unfortunately, I can think of a few things they might have found in there.

"I guess one of the officers needed to use the toilet during the investigation. When he flushed, it overflowed, and a latex glove and a small plastic bag floated to the top. I suspect they caused the clog."

Double crap. I knew I should have buried that stuff.

"Did you know those items were in the toilet?" Andrea asks.

"No," I respond, shaking my head. *Deny it. Be convincing, and deny it. You don't know anything about that.*

Andrea stares at me, probably trying to decide whether I'm telling the truth. "They will attempt to test those items for additional evidence like fingerprints or DNA, although I'm thinking since they've been soaking in water and excrement, they will reveal nothing. But the fact that they exist and were found in the toilet is evidence itself."

A sudden knock disturbs the door, and a woman in uniform opens it, peering inside.

"The judge is ready for you now."

"Thank you. We'll be out in a minute." Andrea swivels to look at me.

"We haven't talked about your pleading or bail, and there isn't time now. When we get inside the courtroom, don't say anything. That's why I'm here. Stand next to me and try to look innocent. There's only one question you'll need to answer from the judge, and that's how you wish to plead. Your response should be 'not guilty.' That's it, okay?"

I nod my head. My mouth and tongue feel paralyzed, but my heart wants to hammer a hole in my chest. As I stand, my knees buckle, and I lose my balance for a moment. I remind myself to keep breathing as I steady my trembling body.

CHAPTER 26

THEN

I dished up the creamy goodness and sat back down across from Grandpa. Eating that ice cream allowed me to overlook that I had lost the first backgammon game. As I savored the delicious dessert, we started another game, and I asked Grandpa about the photo album I had found in the locked cabinet.

"Why do you keep it hidden?"

"I wondered when you'd ask me about that. I guess it should be yours now. All of the pictures are of Athertons."

"I noticed that. My dad and I look a lot alike."

"Yes, you do, but just because you look like him, doesn't mean you'll be like him."

"I know."

"You can follow your own path."

I thought about that for a minute, all the comparisons between fathers and sons. We might look alike on the outside, but we're different people on the inside.

"Is it hard for you to look at photos of Mark?"

Grandpa held the dice and looked at me, sighing. "Yes, it is. I feel the pain and loss all over again when I look at his young face.

It's almost too much to bear. Someday I'll tell you more about that, but not tonight."

"I understand. I want to hear more about the family, but not until you're ready."

As Grandpa rolled the dice and started the next game, he revealed that he went to see a doctor that day. "That's who called this morning, to confirm the appointment. I should've told you then, but I didn't want to make a fuss. I was rude to you, though. You deserved an explanation. I'm sorry."

Aha. The ice cream is part of an apology. It seemed silly not to just tell me he had an appointment, but whatever. We didn't tell each other everything. He had a right to keep his personal matters private.

"It's okay. You made it clear that you were going to town alone. I was mad at first, but I got over it." I tried to act nonchalant, like I didn't care.

Grandpa gave me a look that made me question whether my words were convincing. We continued the game, and I stayed silent, focusing on the board and hoping for some luck with the dice.

"I understand you were angry with me. It was unfair not to bring you along. I've lived alone for so long, sometimes I forget what it's like to consider another's feelings. I want to make it up to you."

"You don't have to do that."

Again, I tried to sound convincing, but my brain itched with the knowledge that I needed to get to Waldport. After today's texts, my conscience was strained, and I felt guilty that I remained shackled to my old life. Even though I'd stayed sober, the past haunted me. *If I mention it to Grandpa, will he understand? Will he call my mom? Will he involve the police? Will he kick me out?*

"Maybe we can go next week," I said casually, advancing two of my checkers.

"Sure, next week is good. We could do something fun, not just get roofing supplies. How about crabbing at the coast or clamming in the bay? Or, we could drive to Newport for some of that knockout chowder?"

Grandpa sounded strangely excited about a trip, like he had visions of taking a vacation day. I hated to burst his bubble, but ulterior motives churned my gut.

"Great," I said, not wanting to get his hopes too high but not having the heart to let him down. "How about Friday?"

"Friday? Weekends are no good. They're crowded. We should pick another day."

"Friday's not the weekend," I sheepishly countered. "We could go to Waldport. It won't be that busy."

"Waldport on Friday?" Grandpa echoed with increasing irritation. "How do you know it won't be overrun with fishermen and tourists and idiots? Summer on the coast is always hectic."

I stayed silent and stared at the board. I hoped to end the game and the conversation by rolling a bunch of double fives or sixes. I felt Grandpa's eyes fixed on me, but I refused to raise mine. Finally, after a tense silence, he relented.

"All right. If that's what you want. We'll go to Waldport on Friday. You haven't been anywhere yet. The least I could do is let you choose when and where we go."

Whew! I completed step one. I chose the date and the destination. Now I had a decision to make about step two. Tell the truth or fabricate a lie. *If I reveal everything to Grandpa about the importance of going to Waldport on Friday, I could lift the weight from my soul. It seems risky, though. I don't want Grandpa involved. But if I make up a story, it might explode in my face, and Grandpa will never trust me again.* I had to tread carefully.

"Friday then?" I confirmed.

"Yup."

"Is it a long trip?"

"Not at all. Didn't you go as a kid?"

"I don't remember."

"It's not far."

"Okay, but maybe you'll be tired. I could go alone?" I mumbled, almost hoping he wouldn't hear me.

"What? Alone? Why would you want to do that?"

I didn't know what to say then. I hadn't planned for our discussion to get that far. The words had just slipped out. I thought I'd have a few days to develop a plan and craft a story. But would Grandpa fall for it? Would he let me drive off on my own? At that moment, I couldn't think of anything to justify my request. I had boxed myself into a corner with only one way out.

"I'm in trouble. I owe somebody lots of money, and if I don't pay him on Friday, he's going to go after Mom."

CHAPTER 27

NOW

I follow Andrea into the courtroom, and it doesn't look anything like the ones I've seen on television. The painted walls lack elegant wood paneling. Simple folding chairs take the place of pews for an audience or the press. It reminds me of a public school classroom with sturdy, industrial folding tables resting on linoleum floors, and that puts me more at ease. The judge, who wears a black robe and looks older than Grandpa, sits at a larger wooden desk, not an elevated throne like in the movies.

Everybody looks up when Andrea and I enter and make our way to the empty table. I settle my nerves by looking down at my hands and then focusing on the flags standing watch in the corner. Besides the judge, several other adults occupy the room, including Deputy Hanson. They huddle together in a tight circle, whispering, and I almost laugh because it looks like that thing football players do.

I also catch a glimpse of a petite woman with sandy brown hair on the far side of the room. My mom sits alone, and when our eyes meet, a flood of shame rushes to my chest. I give her a feeble smile, then look down, swallowing hard as I attempt to remain stoic. I want to run to her and climb into her lap like a little boy who got lost in the woods and craves the safety of his mother's arms.

The bailiff, who led us into the courtroom, interrupts the stillness of the room when she announces, "The Honorable Judge Abner Stevenson presiding."

"Be seated," says the judge, wasting no time. "Who is present today? Please state your names."

"Kent McCormack from the district attorney's office, Your Honor."

"Andrea Salvo from the Office of Public Defense Services, Your Honor, for the defendant, Nash Atherton."

"Thank you. Does the district attorney have a criminal complaint in this matter?"

"Yes, Your Honor. Based on the ongoing investigation, including reports filed by Deputies Hanson and Davis from the county sheriff's department, and pending forensic evidence from the coroner and toxicology lab, our office is prepared to charge Nash Atherton with first degree murder in the death of Fredrick Atherton."

When the words crash into my skull, a bomb explodes, and I desperately want to cry out. Andrea, sensing my shock and horror, grasps my arm and squeezes gently, leaning in to tell me to keep calm. *Keep calm!? How can I do that when I just got shot? I want to panic and run screaming like somebody set my clothes on fire.*

A muffled sob disrupts my thoughts, and I realize my mom also feels the impact of the charge. I hang my head in disgrace, choking back tears. I hadn't really let myself go to this place of worst-case scenarios and impending doom. Until this moment, I didn't think I would actually be accused of murder.

Commotion erupts around me with people talking, pointing fingers, and arguing. I'm left in a stupor, utterly mute. I only snap back to a hazy reality when Judge Stevenson lowers his gavel several times and shouts, "Order in the court!" When the noise dies down, he says in a commanding voice to the attorneys, "We will have time to address all of those issues, but this is my courtroom, and we'll proceed as I see fit."

Everyone settles down, returning to their chairs as the judge continues.

"At this time, will the defendant please rise?"

Like a nurse assisting an invalid, Andrea coaxes me to stand, but I still lean on the table for support.

"In the matter before me, the People of the State of Oregon versus Nash Atherton, you are hereby charged with murder in the first degree. How do you plead?"

The judge stares at me, addressing me directly, but my mind tumbles in a slow-motion dream, leaving me powerless to think or speak or move.

"Mr. Atherton," says the judge, "how do you plead?"

Somehow I manage to mutter a feeble, "Not guilty."

"Let the record show that the defendant has entered a plea of not guilty."

"You can sit down now, Nash," Andrea whispers to me and tugs on my arm. I lower myself onto the chair before I collapse. I feel completely deflated, like someone knocked the air out of my lungs.

"Does the State have a motion for bail?"

"Yes, Your Honor," says the prosecutor. "The State moves that the defendant be held in custody without bail because of his prior criminal record, lack of ties to the community, and lack of employment."

When Andrea jumps to respond, the judge silences her.

"I have a few questions first, Ms. Salvo, and then you will have a turn."

"Yes, Your Honor."

"Mr. McCormack," says the judge. "I understand the defendant is seventeen years old, and his record indicates several recent misdemeanor offenses."

"Yes, Your Honor: possession, vandalism, theft, and disorderly conduct."

"The defendant is currently on probation?"

"Yes."

"And he resides at the home of the deceased, who was his grandfather?"

"Yes, but his official residence is in Portland."

"Has the defendant completed high school?"

"No. He doesn't have a diploma."

"Don't you think it's a stretch to say he's unemployed, when his current job is to finish high school?"

"Yes, Your Honor. I concede that point."

"Okay, Ms. Salvo, what would you like to add?"

"Your Honor, although Nash has a small blemish on his record, he is not a danger to himself or the community. He is a high school student fully capable of completing his degree requirements and has the full support of his mother, Kimberly Atherton. She is prepared to resume full parental responsibility. Nash is an only child, and he has a close relationship with her."

"Your Honor," interrupts the prosecutor, but the judge shuts him down.

"You will have ample opportunity for rebuttal, Mr. McCormack, but it's still the defendant's turn. Ms. Salvo, is Kimberly Atherton present or aware of these proceedings?"

"Yes, Your Honor. She is here in the courtroom today."

Andrea turns and signals for my mom to approach. She hurries to my side, hugging me, kissing my head, and telling me everything will be all right. Her words defy the stress apparent on her face. Her eyes are bloodshot, and worry has etched lines in her forehead and carved dark circles under her eyes. But I relish the warmth of her embrace and feel comforted by the familiar scent of her jasmine perfume.

"Your Honor, I'm Kimberly Atherton, Nash's mother."

"Thank you, Ms. Atherton."

While the judge and my mom talk about where she lives, her job, and why I spent the summer with Grandpa, I keep my focus on her and the prospect that I might not have to stay in jail. I can't believe I haven't seen her in three and a half months. She never came to visit Grandpa and me, even though I invited her several times. I guess she's been busy. She looks tired, and I understand why, but I miss her. I wish she had a little more time for me.

When I started high school, we ate dinner together, watched movies on weekends, and talked regularly about books, sports and school. As I grew older, I spent less time with her and more with my friends. I hope we'll have more time now, because I've always loved her sense of humor and admired her intelligence.

"Thank you, Ms. Atherton and Ms. Salvo. Now, Mr. McCormack, it's your turn. What's on your mind?"

"Your Honor, the State believes the defendant is a danger to himself. Only four months ago he pleaded guilty to several other crimes, and psychologically, we believe he remains at risk. His ties to the community in Portland are also precarious because of his drug use, and his school record is inconsistent at best, showing truancy, academic dishonesty, and failing grades. The State believes it is beneficial and safer for everyone, including the defendant, if he is kept in custody without bail."

"Your response, Ms. Salvo?"

"Your Honor, Nash is willing to undergo a psychological evaluation to demonstrate that he is stable, and not a danger to himself or others. He will also immediately submit a sample for drug testing to show he no longer uses drugs and is not under the influence. If the Court agrees, we move that it is most beneficial for Nash to return to his grandfather's home and reside there with his mother until the estate matters are settled. Nash spent the summer recovering from drug addiction and cultivating an impressive vegetable garden that needs his attention. His mother has agreed to live there with Nash and support him while he earns a Graduate Equivalency Degree."

"Mr. McCormack?"

"Your Honor, this is a murder charge. It is the State's request that the defendant be kept in custody to keep him from disappearing. However, if your Honor is considering bail, the State recommends setting it at five hundred thousand dollars."

"Okay, counselors, let me have a minute to review everything."

CHAPTER 28
THEN

I had never been a salad-eater, but the garden fresh produce changed my palate as I discovered that many vegetables tasted sweet. I felt a sense of accomplishment when I gathered the food, knowing I helped cultivate the bounty. Most days, when I had finished tending the plants, I fished at the river, or explored the area for wild blackberry bushes. By mid-July, the fruit had just started to peak. If you gently pinched the dark, plump orbs and pulled, the ripe ones slid into your hand like a gift from Mother Nature herself.

Grandpa didn't join me in the garden or venture down to the creek as often by then. I noticed a measurable decrease in his energy and activity as he focused on our plan to deal with Carl. Some days he stayed indoors, making phone calls and reviewing paperwork, barely setting foot outside to survey our thriving plot. Other days he took the truck to town for errands or appointments. He informed me of his trips when he departed, but steered clear of any details.

After I confessed to Grandpa about Carl, I felt somewhat relieved, but foolish for having the problem in the first place. Carl had threatened me before, but not with an ultimatum that involved my mom. I detected a hint of desperation in his demand, and it made me uneasy. And then I had shared the burden with Grandpa. *Could we really handle a drug dealer?*

On Thursday night, as we sat studying the backgammon board, Grandpa asked me how I got involved with Carl in the first place. My body stiffened at the inquiry, and Grandpa must have noticed because he softened his tone.

"I mean, how did you meet?"

I relaxed because I knew he meant well. "He's my best friend Eric's older brother. I met him at their house."

Grandpa nodded and rolled the dice. "I see, and is Eric still a friend?"

"I'm not sure," I said, watching Grandpa move his checkers. "I thought he was, but it seems like he's siding with his brother."

"Yes, if they're brothers and they live together, they might also be in business together. If you don't plan to be part of that world, then you're probably not friends anymore."

"I know," I said with a heavy sigh. "That sucks."

"Does it?" asked Grandpa, raising his eyes to look at me, waiting to see if I had more to say. "I won't pretend to know things I don't, but from what your mom divulged, you spent all your time with those boys, using drugs, lying, stealing, and failing in school. You were harming yourself, so I'm not sure that's a relationship you want to keep."

The truth hurts sometimes. Deep down, I knew he was right, but part of me didn't want to let go. I clung to the belief that best friends looked out for each other. I thought we had an unbreakable bond. At the very least, I wanted to separate on my terms.

"I'm not judging," Grandpa continued, in an oddly placid voice. "I only want you to be healthy and happy and have a chance for a long life. If I pay off your debt, which I'm prepared to do, it's not unreasonable for me to want some assurance that the life of drugs is behind you."

I pondered that for a moment: *my life of drugs.* That chapter lasted less than a year. *Did it define me? Did it frame my entire existence? Did it dictate my future?* Of course not, but I sometimes struggled to remember the simpler days when I played outside, read books, competed in sports, and hung out with my family.

"Nash, I'm trying to understand where you've come from so I can help you move in a new direction."

A lump blocked my throat, and the early sting of tears invaded my eyes. I inhaled deeply to calm myself. "I don't want that life anymore, the old one in Portland with drugs and hangovers and lies and secrets. I kind of like this life, here with you."

"My instincts were right then. You do like it here, and you've turned out to be a darn good gardener. Grandma Helen would be extremely proud. I know I am."

"Thanks, Grandpa. I had my doubts at the beginning, that first week I arrived. I was pathetic. I didn't know anything, and I'd never really worked that hard. But I understand things now, about the garden and fishing and what's important."

"That's great to hear, even though I could already see that. From an old man's perspective, there's no downside to hard work. It always pays off somewhere down the line."

My moment of pride and self-respect faded fast, and I suddenly felt guilty because Grandpa said he would pay my debt to Carl. It must have shown in my face because Grandpa quickly reassured me.

"You can't put a price on freedom, Nash, so don't feel bad about the money. This is your chance for a new start, so let's pay up and put this whole mess behind you."

I felt reassured by Grandpa's words and slept surprisingly well that night. I rose at dawn like it was an ordinary day. But, as I fed the chickens and checked the garden fencing, I started to worry about our trip to Waldport. Carl could be unpredictable, and I didn't want trouble.

CHAPTER 29
NOW

While we wait for the judge to make a decision, my mom sits down next to me. I appreciate her love and support, and will do anything, including pee in a cup and see a shrink, if I can get out of here.

"I'm glad you're here, Mom. I'm really scared. I don't know what's going to happen."

"I'm scared, too, but Andrea seems very smart. When she called me yesterday, she explained the whole process. Talking to her made me feel a little better."

"Yeah. I guess you discussed a lot of stuff."

"We did, but preparing for today's hearing was top priority."

"I hope the plan works."

We sit quietly for a few more minutes, while Mom fidgets with her necklace and I bounce my legs, trying to squelch my nervous energy.

"I've reached a decision," says Judge Stevenson, after several minutes of deliberation. I hold my breath and clench my hands into fists, terrified of the words I might hear.

"I order the defendant to be released on bond in the amount of one hundred thousand dollars, into the custody of his mother,

Kimberly Atherton, so they may live at the deceased's home. The defendant will immediately submit a urine sample for drug testing, undergo a psychological evaluation prior to release, and wear an electronic ankle monitor twenty-four hours a day. He may not leave the state of Oregon while wearing the device. A supervising officer will physically check on the defendant once a week, and the defendant can begin studies to earn the equivalent of a high school diploma. I believe any drugs have been confiscated from the premises in question, and the defendant and Ms. Atherton must agree that no drugs, including alcohol, are permitted in the home."

Hearing the word *released* feels like I won the lottery. I exhale the stale air from my lungs and look up toward the ceiling, saying a silent prayer. I don't know what the judge said after that, but I'll do whatever he requires to get out of here.

"That's it for today," continues the judge. "Bailiff, please take the defendant into custody until bail is posted. Counselors, let's set a date for pre-trial motions."

I stand and hug my mom tightly, not wanting to let go. I look at Andrea, and she smiles at me before turning her attention to the judge and a calendar on the table in front of her. As I look at the days and weeks ahead, marked with boxes and numbers, I can only guess when I'll walk out of here.

A few days later, when I leave the courthouse, I realize I haven't been outside in six days. It feels like six years. The warm, moist air fills my nostrils and replenishes my lungs. I gaze up at the blue sky beyond the treetops, feeling the comfort of nature. I have a clunky monitor strapped to my ankle, but the nuisance won't keep me from relishing the freedom of the outdoors.

My mom accompanies me, and the car is packed with her clothes and other belongings. We're ready to drive to Grandpa's house and get settled, pursuant to Judge Stevenson's order.

"We need to stop at the store," says my mom. "There probably isn't much food at Grandpa's."

"There are probably lots of vegetables in the garden," I reply, "but stuff in the fridge might be spoiled."

"What else do you think we need?"

"I don't know."

"Is there any dish soap or laundry detergent?"

"I doubt it."

"How did you clean things?"

"With water."

"We'll get sponges, too, and some bleach."

Living on Drift Creek will be awkward without Grandpa. His aura occupies every nook of the property. I can't be inside the house or out in the yard without thinking of him. But considering the charges hanging over my head, we have to find a way to make it work. Mom used the house in Portland as collateral to obtain a bond for my release. She needs to preserve that asset, and I will do everything in my power to help her.

When we pull into the driveway, the place looks somber, yet serene. Clusters of weeds have sprouted randomly in the gravel, and a few chickens squawk and scurry about. As we unload the car, I'm surprised by what I find.

"What's this?" I say, grabbing an empty wine bottle from under the passenger seat and holding it up for her to see.

"Oh, that. It must be a friend's. We went to a party last week, and she brought some wine."

"Why would an empty bottle be in the car?"

"I guess I was going to recycle it and forgot."

"You weren't drinking, were you?"

"No, Nash. I don't drink."

"Okay, good."

I throw the bottle in the trash, and my mom agrees to tackle the cleaning and straightening inside, while I handle the outside tasks in the garden. When I enter the backyard and survey the plot, everything looks lush, green, and fairly orderly. I can tell it rained during the past week; weeds have sprouted between the rows. But, I don't see any evidence that animals have breached the fence or ransacked the vegetables.

After feeding the hens, I grab a few empty bushels from the shed and get to work. I'll harvest as much as possible today, and promise myself that I'll address the weeds and pests tomorrow. Grandpa's old gloves rest peacefully on the bench, so I slide my hands inside. I half-expect them to feel warm from his skin or damp with sweat, but they're cold, rough and dry. As I bow my head and stare at my hands, a lump fills my throat. I swallow hard and head to the garden.

For the next few days, we go through the motions. Mom does the laundry and the cooking, even though I made some pretty good meals for Grandpa and me. I tend the garden, look after the chickens, and attempt to fix things around the house. Mom goes for walks alone, and I take my usual breaks to go fishing. We lead separate lives, and it bothers me. I'm used to the comfortable rhythm with Grandpa, and I can't help comparing the two.

"I could grill the fish for dinner tonight, and season it with fresh mushrooms and herbs?"

"I've got it, Nash. Let's just bread it and bake it like we always do."

"But that's boring. It's so bland."

"You can grill some other night. I'm sure you'll catch another fish."

After dinner and dishes, I feel restless and ask my mom if she wants to play cards. "How about a game of Crazy Eights?"

"What? A card game?"

"Yeah, unless you want to try to beat me at backgammon?"

"No. I'm tired. I'm turning in early. I only have a few days off, and I need to catch up on my sleep."

"Oh, okay."

"Don't act so dejected. You can play solitaire or read a book or something."

"Sounds fun."

"Have you been reading for that English class?"

"Yes."

"Have you finished any reports and turned them in to your teacher?"

"No. I don't have a computer."

"You don't need a computer. You need pen and paper."

"That's so Stone Age. I'm not doing that."

"Well, then you're going to have to repeat eleventh grade English."

"Whatever."

"It's your choice."

"Fine."

"Good night, Nash."

"Night."

CHAPTER 30
THEN

G randpa and I didn't talk during breakfast. I suppose we were both mulling over the plan to pay off Carl. I hid my anxiety and tried to focus on the positive, on the fact that my debt would be erased.

We left the house early for our half-hour journey and found the grocery store parking lot crowded. We drove around for a few minutes and waited for a space to open near the main doors. Our plan was to stay near the entrance at all times, or go inside the store because security cameras would be rolling. We wanted the transaction recorded in case something went wrong.

While Grandpa went inside for a newspaper, I stayed in the truck, scanning the parking lot for Carl's car. As I waited and watched, my stomach leaped and twisted like a gymnast. When Grandpa returned and opened the driver's side door, he held not only the paper, but also coffee for him and a soda for me. I held the drinks as he climbed into the seat, clutching his chest and groaning at the effort.

When he closed the door, my phone pinged, and we looked at each other knowingly. A message appeared from an unknown number, and I read it out loud.

"Walk to north end of lot. Sidewalk past carts, ATM *and barber."*

I looked up from my phone and said, "I guess that takes away our plan to rely on security cameras."

"Yes, it does," replied Grandpa, sipping his coffee. "I don't like it. What do you want to do?"

I hesitated for a moment, taking a deep breath and blinking hard. I felt like I needed to take charge. "Follow the directions and get this done."

"Okay, Nash. Are we going together like we talked about?"

"No," I said, setting down my unopened root beer. "I should go alone. They know me, and I need to finish what I started."

Grandpa looked at me and nodded. He reached into his pocket and took out an envelope that contained fifteen crisp one hundred dollar bills. "Be careful."

"Thanks," I said, meaning it more than a single word could express. As I opened the passenger door and hopped out, he had a few more words of advice.

"Put that in your pocket. And don't get in the car with them."

"I know," I said, shutting the door.

"And don't turn your back on them," he said, starting the truck.

"I won't, Grandpa."

"I'm gonna drive down that way, but don't look back at me. I want to get eyes on them. If they do anything funny, I'll ram their car."

I turned and marched to the end of the sidewalk, reminding myself that these guys used to be my friends. We hung out together. They didn't carry weapons. They didn't want trouble. My gut told me they just wanted the money. When I stopped and looked to my right, I saw the rusted silver sedan that regularly occupied the driveway at Eric's house. As I proceeded toward it, I could see both

Eric and Carl in the front seat. Neither of them moved, but they watched me as I approached.

I looked at my buddy Eric and barely recognized him. His pale, gaunt face looked sickly, and his empty eyes stared without blinking. He stayed in the car while Carl got out to meet me. From the corner of my eye, I saw Grandpa maneuver his truck in my direction, but I focused on Carl and kept up my poker face, hoping fear didn't reflect back in my eyes.

"Hey, runt, you here alone?"

"Yeah," I said, ignoring the reality that Grandpa wasn't far away.

"You got the money?" Carl asked, striding in front of the car and onto the sidewalk.

"Yup."

"All fifteen?"

I nodded, planting my feet with my arms crossed in front of my chest.

"That a yes?" he rumbled, shoving his hands into his pockets.

"I got the money," I replied, not wanting to upset him. "But I want your word that we're done, and I don't owe you nothing after this."

Although my English teacher would've winced at my grammar, it felt good to spit out the words. Carl glared at me, narrowing his eyes, frowning slightly. I glanced at Eric to see if he'd heard my demand.

"Let's see the green," Carl countered.

"You'll get it," I hissed, "but I need to hear from you that I'm paid up."

We stood there like two villains in an old Western, staring each other down, contemplating a duel. Neither of us budged until Eric chimed in from the open car window.

"Just tell him, Carl. If he pays, he doesn't owe you anymore."

I hadn't heard Eric's voice in a long time, and when it struck my ears, I detected notes of sadness and remorse. We had been through a lot together, and we used to have so much in common. But now our paths had diverged, and we would go our separate ways. I hoped deep down we would remain friends, despite his allegiance to his brother.

Carl flashed his eyes to Eric, but quickly returned his focus to me. "Okay. You pay fifteen now. It's done."

Not realizing I'd been holding my breath, I exhaled with relief and grabbed the envelope from my pocket. I took a few steps forward and firmly deposited the package into Carl's waiting hand.

While Carl counted the bills, I turned my attention to Eric. I wanted to talk to him alone and tell him about all the changes in my life. I missed him and wanted to reconnect and share my good fortune. He gazed at me with a sad, vacant expression, and I understood the emptiness he felt inside. I thought about giving him a hug, and maybe inviting him to live with Grandpa and me, when Carl interrupted.

"It ain't enough, loser. You can get more."

I stared at him while a sneer spread across his face. "What? We had a deal!"

"The deal is you owe more."

"But I paid you. It's all in the envelope."

As I looked to Eric, who was slouching down in the car seat, my eyes pleaded with him to intervene. Before I could speak again, Carl lunged and shoved me to the ground. When I hit the concrete, the toe of his boot slammed into my ribs, and I yelped in pain. While I tried to protect my face and head from the blows, Grandpa emerged from the truck with fire in his eyes, and a loaded cross-bow aimed at Carl's heart.

"You touch him again I'll shoot this right through you."

From my position on the ground, I watched Grandpa set his feet and narrow his eyes, growling like a rabid dog. Carl's eye twitched, and he looked around, taking a small step backward. Grandpa remained focused on his target.

"I've seen men bleed. I've watched them die. One more's not gonna bother me."

The blood drained from Carl's face, and he retreated a few more steps. Grandpa followed him like a hunter tracking prey. In a split second, Carl had slipped back into the car, putting a shield of metal and glass between them. Without warning, he fired up the engine and peeled out of the parking lot. The smell of burnt rubber hung in the air.

Without a word, Grandpa lowered his weapon and extended his hand to help me. Our eyes locked as he hoisted me up. I winced, but said nothing. My immeasurable gratitude was implied.

CHAPTER 31

NOW

S everal days later, Andrea comes by the house to give us an update on the case. I leave my shovel in the garden, and join her and my mom inside for lemonade, sandwiches, and sea salt potato chips. The house looks tidy and smells like lemon thanks to cleaning spray and fresh lavender from the yard. We sit at the kitchen table to eat, and Andrea pulls some files out of her scuffed briefcase. My mom puts her sandwich down on her plate to listen, but my growling stomach compels me to keep eating.

"I have several reports from the forensic lab, but the coroner's report isn't available yet. I also called the doctor listed on the prescription bottle for the medication that was found in the trash. Dr. Robert Baker confirmed that he was the primary care physician for Fredrick Atherton and has been for a long time. He prescribed the Restoril, and told me that Fred had been taking it off and on for several years to help him sleep and alleviate his nightmares."

We let this information sink in for a moment as I attempt to muffle the crunch of the potato chips I'm munching on.

"That's a pretty powerful drug, especially for older people. It tends to stay in their system longer, plus it can be addicting," offers my mom.

"Yes, I did a little research on the medication, and if Fred had been taking it for a while, he might have been addicted."

"I didn't know any of that," I say. "I never saw him take any pills. He just used his inhaler."

"That's fine," says Andrea, "and it's consistent with the absence of your fingerprints on the bottle. The investigators pulled prints, and they all matched your grandfather's. And as expected, no fingerprints were found on the plastic bag or glove in the toilet." Andrea pauses, looking from Mom to me, then continues with a different report. "This, however, is from the forensic lab, where they attempted to determine the contents of the drinking glass and the plastic bag. As Nash told me several days ago, the glass contained water. The lab confirmed that, but it also contained traces of an opioid, not soluble in water. They're going to perform more elaborate tests in an effort to pinpoint exactly what substance was suspended in the water. It might take several weeks."

Neither Mom nor I speak when we hear this information. We both know I experimented with painkillers many months ago, and I stole most of them from her secret hospital stash. I scan my mom's face, which plainly displays a strange, uneasy look. Her lips are pressed together, and her eyes focus downward toward the table. Andrea doesn't seem to notice our mutual concern and continues reading.

"The plastic baggie, which, according to the investigators, was sealed before it ended up in the toilet, also contained minute traces of an opioid. They're going to test that also to see if the substances are identical."

"Okay," my mom says, choosing her words carefully. "So we think Fred was taking pain medication in addition to his sleeping pills?"

"Yes, I think that's a possibility considering the evidence in the reports. I plan to call Dr. Baker and inquire about any other medication he'd prescribed to Mr. Atherton. If he won't speak with me because of the doctor-patient privilege, we will have to wait until the prosecution subpoenas the doctor, and he is forced to testify."

I stop eating and slouch down in my chair, glancing from Andrea to my mom. I hope this meeting ends soon. My hunger has disappeared, and my mind races. My legs start to bounce as I stare out the window. This would be an opportune time to retreat to the garden. I don't want to hear any more about Grandpa or the evidence. I want to escape all of it and take a walk by the creek, or go fishing. Part of me knows I should stay and tell Andrea and my mom about the night of August seventeenth. But something stops me, tells me I ought to keep quiet.

As the silence stretches beyond a comfortable pause, Andrea takes the hint, shuffles the papers one more time, and focuses on a different report. "They also discovered Fred's blood on the doorframe, wall and floor outside the bathroom. Nash already told me about that."

"Yeah, Grandpa was unsteady. He probably could have used one of those old people walker things."

"I wish you had told me that, Nash," says my mom. "I could've bought him one and had it shipped to the house."

"If you sent him one, he would've ignored it. Besides, most of the time he was fine. He would hang onto a chair or lean against the wall when he needed extra support."

"I think the evidence will show that Fred simply hit his head after he stumbled and fell," says Andrea.

"That's what happened," I say.

"And they didn't find any blood on the tools the police confiscated from the kitchen or the shed."

"That's good," I say.

"I agree. They haven't found a 'weapon,' per se."

"What a relief," adds my mom.

"They also gathered several hairs from the rug in the living room and determined they came from Grandpa, and both of you."

"They found our hair?" I ask.

"Yes," Andrea replies.

"Grandpa's, Mom's and mine?"

"Yes. Do you think that's odd?"

I glance at my mom for a moment, but I can't quite read the look on her face. *I don't know what I'm supposed to say. Yes, it is odd because she never came here.*

"I'm sure Kimberly visited during the past few months. With long hair like ours, one or two strands always seem to fall out," says Andrea.

"Right," says my mom, nodding her head. "That's what I told the police. I stopped in whenever I could to see how things were going. We often sat in the living room and talked."

"Did the police contact you for an interview?"

"Yes, several days after Grandpa's death. Didn't I tell you?"

"No, and I don't see that in the file. Actually, I don't see any witness information in the file."

"It's probably because I didn't have much to tell them. I knew the summer was going well for Nash, but Fred was sick. I checked on them every other week or so, when my schedule was open."

I stare at my mom with a frown. *She's lying. Why is she lying?* She didn't visit at all this summer. *And she lied to the police? That seems crazy.*

"The hair isn't a big deal, except for the lack of other hairs. Like the fingerprints, it's circumstantial evidence that no one else appears to have been inside the house," explains Andrea.

I lock eyes with my mom and she shrugs her shoulders, then runs her hand over the top of her head.

"Okay," say Andrea. "I'll share this one final report before I go, but I have to warn you, it will be difficult to hear."

Andrea looks ominously from me to my mom. My mouth goes dry. I can feel my heart beating inside my chest, pounding relentlessly against its cage. I don't want to hear what Andrea's going to say next, but I have no choice. Andrea fixes her attention on me.

"They found the bloody towels in the garden."

"They found what!?" shrieks my mom.

I know what Andrea is talking about, but my mom doesn't. Without a word, I get up from the table and step outside. I'd been in the garden every day since my release, but I hadn't noticed someone dug up the towels. *How could I have missed that*? I guess I had been avoiding that patch. When I reach the spot, the area looks lightly trampled. I pull back the squash leaves and find the freshly turned dirt.

My mom and Andrea follow me outside. Mom reaches me first, and I know what she's going to say.

"What were you thinking?"

"I don't know."

"Why did you do that? It makes you look guilty."

"I panicked. The bloody towels looked so horrible. I just wanted to get rid of them."

"You could have washed them."

"I didn't think of that. Besides, we didn't have any detergent, and who knows if blood comes out with water."

"Oh my god, Nash. They're going to pin this on you."

"Get a grip, Mom. They're just towels. I can explain it. Right, Andrea?"

"We'll certainly try, but it won't be easy."

We stand there for a few moments, staring at the dirt.

"What about this?" I suggest. "Grandpa told me that after hunting he liked to spread the blood of his kill on the soil. He offered it back to the earth, expressing his gratitude by saying a prayer. That's kinda what I did."

"Interesting. Is that some kind of ritual?" asks Andrea.

"It might be a Native American practice," I say and shrug. "Grandpa had a lot of respect for the area's native people."

"I can do a little research on it when I get home."

"Oh, for Chrissakes, that's reaching."

"Come on, Mom. It's better than nothing."

"Nash is right. It's a peculiar explanation, but we'll see if we even get to that point."

We're quiet for a few more minutes, and then Andrea turns to look at me. "If you buried anything else, I don't want to know about it."

She leaves the garden, making her way back to the house. My mom stares at me for a few minutes and shakes her head, then retreats, too. I remain rooted to the spot, more at home among the plants and earthworms.

CHAPTER 32

THEN

Even with bruised ribs, I couldn't recall ever feeling so buoyant. Grandpa and I celebrated my freedom from Carl by driving to the dunes to enjoy the sunshine, then feasting on Dungeness crab and creamy clam chowder. The payoff hadn't gone like we expected, but I still felt tremendous relief. The people in my past, and any former drug use, no longer ruled my life. My release from those chains would have been impossible without Grandpa's help, and almost everything in my life seemed positive that day.

Despite my happiness and feeling of liberation, though, I also felt conflicted. I was sorry to see Eric ensnared in that dirty business with his brother. *Could I have helped him? Why hadn't I reached out earlier?* As I thought about it, my heart ached more than my abused ribs. I knew deep down. *I couldn't help him. I couldn't comfort him. I couldn't save him from himself.*

When we arrived at the house, Grandpa went inside to rest. I left all thoughts of Eric and Carl behind as I tackled a few chores in the yard. I felt robust and energetic, like a man who had found his purpose in life. That evening, I started writing an almanac to record the gardening events as a guide for next year. Somehow, I wanted to continue this lifestyle of relative self-sufficiency, living off the land, and trusting myself.

"Grandpa, do you think we could expand the garden a little?"

"What would you add?"

"Maybe I wouldn't add to the garden, but what about planting some raspberries and blackberries on the other side of the shed? It would be nice to have fruit to pick every summer."

"Those bushes grow like weeds."

"We could start small with just one or two. I could trim them and keep them under control."

"Okay, I don't see why not."

"And maybe we could get a goat for the yard."

"A goat? Wouldn't you rather have a dog?"

"Well, yeah, a dog would be great, but a goat could keep the grass trimmed and provide milk."

"Have you looked into this?"

"No, not really, but I thought we could supplement the fishing catch, vegetables, and eggs with goat's milk."

"You know a goat has to be pregnant to produce milk."

"Oh, I didn't think about that. Maybe it isn't such a good idea."

"Probably not."

"Do you think you could teach me to hunt then?"

"I'm sorry, Nash, but I'm getting too old and slow for that."

"Are you sure?"

"My old bones can't take it anymore, but I can check with Earl. He might take you hunting."

"You mean your scary neighbor?"

"Yup, he's a skilled hunter. You could learn a lot from him."

"I don't know, Grandpa. He kinda gives me the creeps."

"He's not scary if you get to know him."

"Okay. I'll think about it."

As I worked around the property and dreamed of my ideal life, Grandpa stayed on the sidelines more and more. He deferred to my judgment and took orders from me. I organized the workdays and made suggestions for improvements. When he listened to my opinions, it buoyed my confidence. In a few weeks, I could barely believe it when the calendar turned from July to August.

I noticed Grandpa's daily activities slowed during that time. He rarely set foot in the garden anymore. He went to bed earlier than usual and slept well after sunrise. He sometimes went down to the creek during the day and returned without a single fish. I pretended to ignore it, but his lack of effort annoyed me. We argued because I felt like Grandpa failed to carry his weight. How would we get my plans off the ground if he didn't contribute?

"What's wrong with you?" I asked him one evening, irritated when he shunned my request to help clean the kitchen after dinner.

"I'm tired," he said as he shuffled into the living room and dropped himself into the worn chair.

"How can you be tired?" I said, exasperated by his lame excuse. "You didn't do anything today."

He wheezed out a sigh and started to reply, but instead of words, he ended up doubled over and blindsided by a coughing fit. It reminded me of a kid at school who had asthma, and when he coughed, he would turn blue because he couldn't breathe. I paused in the kitchen and brought Grandpa some water. When I placed my hand on his back for support, the bones of his spine felt like a skeleton.

"Are you sick, Grandpa? Do you have bronchitis?"

"Can you get my inhaler?" he whispered, gasping for air. "It's by the bed."

I proceeded to his room and spied it on the low wooden table next to the bed. In a short time, Grandpa breathed easier, but still struggled as the redness in his face faded to pink. After he'd had a few minutes to recover, I inquired again, but this time with genuine concern.

"Are you sick?"

"Yeah. I went to the doctor yesterday, and I got bronchitis, so I need this," he said, waving the inhaler in his hand.

"Well, that explains a lot," I said, returning to the kitchen to finish the dishes. "You haven't been working much lately, and we're falling behind in the garden."

"Maybe I can help next week."

"Next week?" I said, trying hard to hide my frustration. "There's going to be a lot of vegetables to harvest soon, and we need to fix the door on the chicken coop and patch the roof before it rains again."

"I know I ain't much help," he said gruffly.

After a while, a chilly silence settled between us.

"Do you want to play backgammon?" I asked in an attempt to thaw the ice.

"Not tonight. I'm going to bed."

Without looking at me, Grandpa stood and gritted his teeth, as if he exerted the same effort as a weightlifter hoisting a giant barbell. He looked unsteady on his feet, and teetered for a moment with his back hunched, eyes staring at the floor. He plodded toward the bedroom, like a laborer carrying sacks of cement. My eyes followed him with both curiosity and alarm until he disappeared around the corner.

Grandpa acted like a completely different person. The man I met three months ago barked orders, dug holes for fence posts, and swung an axe like a lumberjack. This man hid indoors and slept as many hours as a cat. A nagging voice inside me said to check with my mom, even though he had seen a doctor and had medication for his cough. As a nurse, she could tell me how to help him.

In the meantime, the burden of work shifted to me. During the next few days, I'd have to prioritize the tasks around the house and keep a schedule to stay organized. Despite the added responsibility, I knew I could handle the job.

CHAPTER 33

NOW

When I trudge back inside the house, Andrea is in the bathroom, and my mom paces in the kitchen. Her face is red and blotchy. She is shaking her head, muttering to herself. "I don't understand you, Nash."

"What does that mean?"

"Why do you do such stupid things?"

"I don't need this right now, Mom. It's hard enough with you on my side. If you turn on me, then it's going to be impossible."

"I'm not turning on you. I'm just baffled."

"I'm not perfect, okay? You of all people know that."

"I know. None of us is, but you seem to lack common sense."

"Well, shit. Tell me what you really think."

"I'm sorry. I'm just worried."

I nod faintly, thinking back to the night before Grandpa died.

"I didn't want him to die," I say, my poker face suddenly collapsing into sobs of guilt and grief. "I wanted to call an ambulance or go to the ER for stitches. He refused. He was so confused and weak. He told me to leave him alone and go to bed. I don't know if I did the right thing."

"Oh, honey. That must have been hard for you."

"I wanted to get him some help."

"I know, you loved Grandpa and were trying to help him."

Andrea joins us in the kitchen with a different mindset. "Do the police have any reason to believe you wanted him dead?"

"What?" exclaims my mom, tears flooding her eyes. "That's absolutely crazy. They cared about each other. They loved each other."

"Kimberly," says Andrea, interrupting my mom. "I know you're upset and worried and surprised by all of this, but right now, I need to hear from Nash. He told me they argued."

"Doesn't everyone argue?"

"Nash, did you argue with your grandpa the night he hit his head?"

"Um, no, not that night. Why does it matter?"

"I have a hunch or a theory about what the police might be looking for," says Andrea.

"They won't find any weapons or anything else with blood on it."

"Nash, why is there a hole in this wall?"

We turn and look at the kitchen wall. The pit is a little larger than a fist and about shoulder high.

"I, uh, geez. If you have to know, I punched it."

"I haven't mentioned it, but a photo of that hole is included in the police file."

"What does that mean?" asks my mom.

"It means they think Nash has a temper problem. He likes to punch things."

"I don't follow."

"Do you follow, Nash?"

"Sort of. I have a bit of history punching things."

"Like what?"

"The window of our house, the mailboxes when I was messed up that night I passed out, the orderly in the hospital, and now this wall."

Andrea then turns her attention back to me. "It's not too much of a stretch to think you might have pushed or shoved your grand-father against the wall, but only if they find a motive."

When I open my mouth to respond, someone pounds on the door, interrupting our discussion. We stand paralyzed for a moment, staring at each other. We aren't expecting visitors today. My heart accelerates, and my instincts tell me to flee because the forceful blows sound like the ones issued by the police. I fear they will handcuff me and haul me back to jail. My mom recovers first and peeks out the window. Sensing the person outside means no harm, she steps toward the door and opens it a sliver.

"Who's there?" she asks, her voice a pitch higher than normal.

"It's your neighbor, Earl Fiske."

We relax a bit when we hear the deep, gravelly voice on the other side of the door. Mom opens it wide to reveal a gray-haired man in overalls standing on the stoop. I recognize him immediately. Mom welcomes him inside with a brief hug, and offers him some lemonade, while Andrea and I say hello. He looks a lot older than I remember, and not nearly as menacing without a shotgun.

"I'm checking on Fred to see if he liked the package I left for him."

"Oh? What kind of package was it?" asks Andrea.

"Um, well, it's small, and it's personal. I left it in the mailbox. I been calling the last couple days, but there's no answer."

"That's because Fred passed away."

An awkward silence follows while my mom and I bow our heads.

"Oh. I'm so sorry to hear that," he says, his face downcast. "My condolences. When did he die?"

"More than a week ago," says Andrea. "Were you friends? Did you check on him often?"

I notice Earl shift his eyes to my mom before he returns his gaze to Andrea. "We been friends a long time: since he and Helen bought the place."

"And you visit him regularly?"

"We used to fish together and do some hunting every year."

"When was the last time you saw him?" Andrea asks, pressing for more details.

"I don't remember," he says, scratching his beard. "A couple weeks ago, maybe more. I brought him some venison and another package to try. I talked to him on the phone a few times recently, though. How'd he die?"

I stiffen when he asks this question, and I notice my mom straightens her posture and clenches her jaw. Andrea's face remains expressionless as she responds.

"We're not sure, but I'm surprised you haven't heard. If you're a neighbor, I believe a sheriff's deputy stopped by your house on Saturday, August eighteenth."

Earl doesn't reply immediately. His eyes drift around the kitchen, lingering on my mom again, as he selects his words with caution.

"Is that what the sheriff came by to talk about? I went hunting that day, and nobody's tried to reach me since."

As Mom and I remain still, Andrea continues probing.

"Do you have some information about Fred that you plan to share with the police?"

Earl's eyes are wide like saucers, and his eyebrows rise an inch as he glances from Andrea to my mom. "Are the cops here?" he asks Andrea.

"No," she says in a soothing voice, "it's just us."

"Okay," he says, with a sigh of relief. "I do have some information that I think ya should hear, but I don't want no trouble with police. I can't have 'em coming to my house, looking around, and asking questions. Know what I mean?"

Earl glares at me this time, and I understand. *His marijuana crop isn't legal.*

"What do you think we should hear?" Andrea asks.

"It's a recording on my answering machine. Fred called me the night before he died."

CHAPTER 34
THEN

The muggy days of August came and went, and even though the sun could have beckoned the most stubborn hermit outside, Grandpa stayed indoors. He occupied his favorite chair, reading or dozing, depending on his mood. I toiled in the garden and around the house, but managed to find time to enjoy fishing before sunset.

Grandpa's health didn't improve like he said it would, and I watched his strength and energy vanish in a few short weeks. He dragged his body around the house, leaning on the walls or gripping the back of a chair for support. When he stopped to rest during these short journeys, he clutched his chest, wheezing and gasping for breath. Bending to pick vegetables in the garden or pull weeds in the yard became impossible. Even the peaceful joy of fishing evaporated like a distant memory.

I remained hopeful at first that his illness would pass, and he would make a full recovery, returning to our life that revolved around the garden and the creek. After two weeks, as he struggled to move and breathe, I doubted his condition would improve. I felt the worry like a ticking bomb in the pit of my stomach. I didn't have the courage to ask him about it, though, and the optimist in me believed if I stayed busy and did the work for both of us, he might still rebound. Grandpa remained stoic and volunteered scant information about his health, but it was obvious he was suffering. One evening, I called to consult with my mom about the situation.

"Grandpa isn't getting better. He's still sick."

"Yeah, it takes old people longer to recover from sickness than young people."

"I know, but it seems like he's getting worse."

"Getting worse, yeah, that can happen, too. Getting worse."

"Are you saying it's fine that he's getting worse?"

"No, not fine he's getting worse. He's getting older, not worser."

"What? Grandpa has trouble breathing and walking and stuff. I think he's really sick."

"Yeah, he's sick and having trouble with stuff. You're taking care of him."

"Mom? You sound weird. Why are you slurring your words?"

"I not slurring, just tired. Long day and all."

"Is something wrong?"

"No wrong, good. All good."

"Are you drunk?"

"No, not drunk. I don't drink no more."

"Oh, my god. You're frickin' drunk. You're supposed to be sober."

"I's sober and tired, just tired. Really tired, so I better go."

The line went dead. *What was going on?* She wasn't any help at all. Damn it! *What was I supposed to do?*

I did the only thing I could think of. I took care of Grandpa by cooking and cleaning and sitting with him in the evenings. We talked, and I laid out my ambitious plans for the property. He sat quietly and listened, nodding his head from time to time, asking an occasional question. He never objected or corrected me. Instead, he let me weave a fantastical tale on the loom of his land. One evening, as I discussed my almanac and requested more information about planting times for next season, Grandpa interrupted and changed the subject.

"You know I'm sick," he said, swallowing hard and reaching a feeble hand toward the glass of water next to him. I stopped writing in my notebook, annoyed that he'd broken my train of thought, but gave him my full attention. After taking a sip and setting it back down, Grandpa continued. "I can't live like this anymore, with no energy and constant pain." He paused to catch his breath. "I'm done. I want to end it."

"What do you mean you're done? We're just getting started with our plans for next season."

"You heard me." His dull eyes and deliberate voice conveyed a clearer message than the words themselves.

"No," I said, shaking my head. "You can't be done. There are still things to do and life to live."

"I appreciate everything you've done around here, Nash. I couldn't have asked for a better grandson."

"But there's still hope," I pleaded as my throat tightened. "Let's get you to another doctor for better medicine or a different treatment or something."

"I have a final favor to ask, Nash. Can you do one last thing for me?"

"Well, of course, Grandpa. I'll do anything for you, but let's not talk like that. Will you try to get more help?"

"I'm beyond help. What I need are painkillers."

I sat silently for a moment, puzzled by the request. "You mean you want me to pick up a prescription for you?"

"No prescription. Painkillers. Can you get me some?"

"Like on the street?" *Did I understand correctly? Did he want me to contact Carl, the dealer we had worked so hard to get away from?*

"Yes, I need them."

"Wouldn't it be simpler for your doctor to prescribe something? I'm sure he would do it. You're clearly in pain."

"No more doctors."

"Come on, Grandpa. We can call in the morning, and I'll take you."

"I ain't gonna see more doctors!" he said, raising his voice to a level of fury I hadn't witnessed in months. Just as quickly, as if he was exhausted by his outburst, he regained his composure and softly pleaded. "Can you get me some?"

It felt like a slap in the face. *Why would he ask me to step back into that illicit world when a doctor could prescribe the medication?* I sat perfectly still and closed my eyes. My head drooped and my heart sank like a lead weight. *If I refused his request, I would forever disappoint him. I had just told him I'd do anything for him. And if I agreed to get the drugs, my actions could jeopardize everything I'd worked for to stay sober and out of trouble.*

After an eternal silence with Grandpa's eyes locked on me like a target, I took the easy way out. I told him what he wanted to hear.

"Yeah. I'll see what I can do."

CHAPTER 35
NOW

In early September, I return to the courthouse with Andrea. She filed a motion to dismiss the case against me because of a lack of evidence, and I hope the judge agrees. I want to be a teenager again, finish high school, and decide what to do with my life.

As the bailiff asks us to rise, and Judge Abner Stevenson enters the room, I glance over my shoulder at my mom. She looks nervous, biting her nails in the spectator area in back. When we sit, Andrea remains standing to address the court.

"Your Honor, this case should be dismissed because the autopsy report lists overdose by accident or suicide as the cause and manner of death. Despite the trauma to his head, and the giant tumor encasing his lungs, the medical examiner determined that narcotics killed Fredrick Atherton."

I listen closely as she continues. Grandpa died at 2:45 a.m., and the toxicology report showed evidence of barbiturates, opiates and tetrahydrocannabinol in his body. Together, those substances would induce a deep sleep, stop a person's breathing, and end someone's life.

"There is no probable cause to believe that Nash committed a crime."

The prosecutor McCormack jumps to his feet with a rebuttal. "Your Honor, the report by the medical examiner is inconclusive as to whether the victim died as a result of an accident or suicide. The police did not find a note indicating the latter. I believe we still have a case against the defendant. He remains under investigation and may have supplied the fatal dose of drugs. Although the deceased had a prescription for the barbiturate, he did not have one for the pain-killers. The quantity found in his bloodstream will likely show that opiates were the primary cause of death. I am requesting further toxicology studies on this matter. It is my belief that the deceased may not have acted alone in putting together this drug cocktail."

He pauses for a breath and looks at me. I meet his gaze then focus my attention on the judge before he continues speaking. "In addition, Your Honor, the medical examiner stated the head wound was severe. The deceased may have been shoved against the wall. We have reason to suspect the defendant may be violent. My office wants to continue its investigation of these findings."

"Mr. McCormack," replies Judge Stevenson. "I appreciate your dedication and perseverance in this matter, but I believe it would be a waste of money to run further tests. If the medical examiner suspected homicide, or foul play of any kind, I'm certain he would have listed that as the manner of death, but that's not the case here."

"Yes, Your Honor, I understand, but I also have the alleged last will and testament of Fredrick Atherton, handwritten only days before his death. It directs that his entire estate be given to Nash Atherton. We need time to analyze the handwriting because it could be a fraud, but I believe the untimely death of the will's author is sufficient evidence that foul play existed. The defendant had ample motive to kill his grandfather."

"I see where you're going, Mr. McCormack. A motive would be important if we were headed to trial, but this court cannot ignore the fact that you have presented zero hard evidence that the defendant was culpable in Mr. Atherton's death. There is nothing to indicate that he either supplied the drugs or forced the deceased to take them. The scenario appears to be either a deliberate act by a dying man, or an unfortunate accident."

Andrea remains quiet, listening attentively and taking notes, letting the prosecutor and judge spar with each other.

"Your Honor, the State thinks it's best for the defendant to remain in supervised release while we further investigate these matters, particularly the handwriting and the source of the narcotics. He is already on probation, so it's not a stretch to keep him monitored."

"Ms. Salvo, do you have a response to that request?"

"Yes, Your Honor. As the court knows, the drug test taken by Nash after arraignment was negative. The psychological evaluation administered shortly thereafter was positive. Nash is in good health and of sound mind. He intends to live with his mother and finish high school. If the court plans to dismiss the charges against him in this case, I believe there is no valid reason for him to remain supervised."

"Your Honor," interrupts the prosecutor, "neither of those tests addresses the issue of cause in this case, and whether the defendant contributed to Mr. Atherton's demise."

"Counsel," interrupts the judge. "I've heard enough. You've made your point clear, but I've reached a decision. The State may continue its investigation if that's what the DA deems proper, but Ms. Salvo, I hereby grant your motion to dismiss for lack of evidence. This case is dismissed without prejudice. The defendant shall report to the bailiff for immediate removal of the monitoring device. The State may bring other charges later, but Nash Atherton is free to go."

As Judge Stevenson lowers his gavel, my mom squeals with

excitement, and the thrill of victory flows through my body. I pump my fist and turn to hug Andrea, who has a giant grin on her face. Her guidance through this ordeal has been crucial. My mom joins us and wraps her arms around me. She says we have to go out and celebrate, and I agree. I need to do something fun because the last month has been agony, and I just want to put it all behind me.

When my ankle is free, I turn to exit the courtroom, but the prosecutor waits for me by the door. He blocks my path with his body and speaks in a voice that sounds like the hiss from a snake. "This isn't over, Nash. My investigation is going to continue. I have a very low tolerance for punks who abuse their elders. We'll keep digging, and we'll find the evidence to bury you."

I stare at him, hearing his words, and feel the blood retreat from my face. Andrea notices the confrontation and steps between us.

"Don't harass my client, McCormack. Just because you lost your last three cases doesn't mean you can take it out on him."

"It's just a friendly warning to your client. I'm here to protect the public, and I'm going to win this one."

"Not if I can help it."

I appreciate my lawyer's intervention, relieved to have a competent shield. Andrea escorts me out of the courtroom and tells me to ignore him, but McCormack's words weigh heavily on my mind.

CHAPTER 36
THEN

As Grandpa's physical condition worsened, I stressed about whether to contact Carl to buy some painkillers. The debate ran through my head on an endless loop as I tried to decide what to do. After Grandpa made the request, I couldn't keep it a secret, so I called my mom for advice.

"Grandpa asked me to get him some painkillers. I don't know if I should do it."

"He asked you what? Why would he do that?"

"He says he wants to end it. I think he means the pain, but he might mean something else."

"End it? Has he talked to his doctor?"

"I think so. But he says he's done with doctors. He wants me to help him."

"I don't think that's a good idea. Just keep doing what you're doing. Make him comfortable and take care of things around the house, but nothing more."

"But I promised I would help. I can't go back on my word."

"That's crazy, though. Ignore his request. I'll talk to him. He'll understand. He's asked too much of you."

"But I know him. He's miserable. He wouldn't ask if he thought it was too much."

"Where does he think you'll get painkillers anyway?"

"I know somebody who might be able to help."

"Are you doing to get involved with drugs again?"

"No, it's not like that."

"Don't be foolish, Nash. Leave that stuff to the doctors."

"Okay, if you say so, but he needs help."

"I know. I'll call him."

"I really don't want to disappoint him."

"You won't. It's the right decision to protect yourself first and take care of Grandpa in other ways."

She said he would understand and made it seem so simple. But I had to live with my choice. The prospect of going back on my word plagued me and kept me awake at night.

To my dismay, Grandpa gradually stopped talking to me. His avoidance reminded me of a turtle withdrawing into its shell. I tried to act normal and ask him questions or tell him about the garden, but he either turned his back or pretended he couldn't hear me. I yelled for him to pay attention, but he closed his eyes and sat like a stone statue. I begged and pleaded, but he stared at the newspaper, oblivious to my frustration. He also refused to touch the backgammon board. After a few days of that, I was ready to walk out and never look back.

Later in the week, after an endless day of chores, I returned to the house with a bushel of fresh vegetables. Grandpa rested in his usual place but looked up when I walked inside.

"Is there any venison left?"

I opened the refrigerator to find out. "Yeah. There's one large steak. We can share it."

"Good. You know how I like it."

"Grilled medium rare, and I'll cook some of the beans I picked today."

"Sounds good. Any mushrooms?"

"I gathered some the other day. They'll be great with the meat."

Grandpa didn't eat much of his meal, but I savored the morsels of venison, the final chunk of meat in the house. The next time I wanted some, I might have to buy it at a grocery store. I tried to make conversation during dinner, but Grandpa remained silent, lost in his thoughts. Afterward, he plodded to his chair, and I cleared the table, preparing to wash the dishes. I felt encouraged that Grandpa had at least taken an interest in the meal.

As I cleaned, a guttural groan erupted from the other room. I turned and watched as Grandpa rose from his chair and dragged himself toward the hall. Either his bed or the toilet beckoned, typical for after the evening meal. Several minutes passed before a heavy *thunk* interrupted my work, and I rushed to investigate.

I found Grandpa on his hands and knees in the hallway outside the bathroom. Warm blood flowed from the side of his head. I grabbed a towel for the wound, and helped him up, wondering if he preferred his bed or the chair. His eyes looked glassy, and he seemed confused. I tried to convince him he needed to go to the emergency room for stitches, but he refused.

"Patch me up so I can continue with the platoon," he commanded.

I played along and helped him to the chair. Once he was seated, I followed orders and absorbed the blood with the towel.

"Hurry up, I've got to stay with my men."

I left him for a moment to check the bathroom cabinets for bandages or something to clean the cut.

"Be alert for snipers on the hill!" he called after me.

Had Grandpa suffered a concussion? He mumbled about hurrying up, taking cover, and staying quiet, like a soldier in the war. When he eventually dozed off, I cleaned up most of the dried blood, but the laceration on his head continued draining, even after I applied pressure.

I thought about going to bed but knew I should stay with Grandpa. I called my mom to ask her about treating a head wound, and she instructed me to keep him alert. Following her advice, I nudged Grandpa, coaxing him awake. He opened his eyes and stared at me for a long time as I whispered to him, asking him how he felt, if he remembered what happened.

"Thank you for everything," he said, ignoring my questions.

"You need to see a doctor, Grandpa. The cut on your head is serious."

"It's fine for tonight. We can take care of it tomorrow."

I didn't argue with him because he sounded coherent now, and made it clear he didn't want me fussing over him.

"Okay, if you're sure. Do you need anything?"

"Some water?"

"Of course," I said, and went to the kitchen for a glass. When I set it down next to him, he reached out and clutched my hand, pulling me close.

"I have a confession to make, Nash."

I hunched over him and listened. His grip tightened as he started to speak.

"I blamed Jeff for his brother's death, but I've known all along it wasn't his fault."

We didn't talk about my father very often, and nobody ever talked about his older brother Mark. Now Grandpa wanted to tell me, and I inched closer so I could hear him clearly.

"Jeff got a hold of my gun, and Mark tried to take it away from him. The gun went off and shot Mark in the head." Tears ran down Grandpa's pale, wrinkled face as he recalled the events of that day.

I felt the heaviness in his heart as he divulged his most painful memory. "The paramedics came, but it was too late."

"That's awful, Grandpa."

"I always blamed Jeff, but it was my fault. He was only eight."

The disclosure hit me like a punch in the face. *How do you respond to learning that your dad killed his own brother? That kind of tragedy haunts a family for life. I could see how Grandpa blamed my dad because he held the gun. But Grandpa's loaded weapon did the killing, and he carried the weight of that knowledge all those years.* I remained silent for a long time, processing the information, wondering how anyone lived with that kind of burden. Then I realized my dad couldn't. The horror of that day and the guilt he harbored eventually defeated him.

"I'm sorry," I said, and leaned in to embrace Grandpa. What else could I say to a man who lost both of his sons?

"Thank you," he said, and we left it at that.

Grandpa wanted to stay in the chair for a while and told me to go to bed. I felt tired and knew tomorrow would be a long day if we added an emergency room visit to the schedule.

"Okay, Grandpa. If you're feeling all right, I'll go to bed."

"Good night, Nash."

"Good night, Grandpa."

CHAPTER 37
NOW

When Mom and I leave the courthouse, we drive west toward the coast. I can't decide whether I want a giant cheeseburger or deep-dish pizza, so we giddily agree to have both. During the ride, I stare out the window, watching the sparkling blue water of the Pacific Ocean creep into view. I try to forget about McCormack's warning and focus on dipping my feet into the frigid water and feeling the sand caress my toes.

After stuffing ourselves with food, we wander along an empty beach, looking for driftwood and sea glass. I lose myself in my thoughts, thankful the nightmare has ended, but grief-stricken about Grandpa's absence. *He should be here.* When Mom and I stop to admire the landscape, a few curious seagulls join us. The isolation compels me to make a final confession. I reveal what my mom might already suspect.

"I supplied the painkillers to Grandpa."

"Nash! I thought we talked about that and agreed it was a bad idea."

"I know."

"You said you would take care of him and keep him comfortable, not buy drugs for him."

"I'm sorry," I wail, as tears stream down my face. "I couldn't break my promise. He asked for them, and I thought it would help ease his pain. I didn't expect this. I didn't want him to die."

"I know, but you put yourself at risk. Where did you get those painkillers?"

"From a friend."

"In Portland?"

"Yes, but I'm not going to tell you the details. It was a one-time deal."

"Oh my god. I hope you're right. If the police start poking around, you could go back to jail."

"I know, but it might help if they heard Grandpa's voicemail message to Earl. Maybe we should ask him to save it?"

"That's a good idea. I recorded it when Earl played it for us, but it's probably more authentic if it's saved on his answering machine."

"You recorded it?"

"Yes, on my phone. When Earl invited us over to listen to the message, I guess you and Andrea were so focused on Grandpa's words that you didn't notice."

"Will you play it for me now? I want to hear Grandpa's voice one more time."

"Are you sure?"

"Yes."

"*Hey Earl, it's Fred. I got your package. I'll give it a try. You know I can't go hunting with you. The cancer is making it impossible to do anything and I'm done with all the nonsense. I wanted you to know. I'm gonna end it soon. I'll miss my grandson, Nash, but he'll be all right. He's smart and strong and resilient. He made these last few months some of the best of my life. Well, that's all. It's been nice knowing you. Goodbye, Earl.*"

My mom holds me while I cry, releasing a torrent of stress and sadness. I haven't allowed myself to feel any grief about Grandpa's death. During the past weeks, I've been holding it all in, and now, it gushes out of me like water from a hydrant. I miss him so much, more than I ever thought I would, and I wish I had more time with him.

My mom attempts to comfort me, hugging me, telling me she understands.

"You made a difficult decision. It wasn't necessarily a smart one, but at least Grandpa is in a better place. I believe he is at peace with Grandma Helen."

"I know, but I feel guilty about what I did."

"Try not to think about that. You honored his request. And hopefully they can't trace those pills to you."

"I just wish I had told him I loved him."

"He knew that. I'm sure of it."

"I hope so."

"Things will get better. You'll see. It will take time, but we'll adjust to life without him."

Her words seem hollow and do nothing to relieve my heartache. I don't want to adjust to life without him. Grandpa had filled the hole left by my dad, and now I feel empty and alone again.

CHAPTER 38

THEN

My eyes sprang open when the toilet flushed. I found the noise odd because Grandpa never got up early anymore. In my haste to check on him, I kicked a small pile of books, and the thud disrupted the quiet of the house.

As I searched the darkness for my pants, my ears alerted me to a faint creaking noise, like someone walking across the wood plank floor. When I turned on the bedroom light and opened my door to investigate, the front door slammed, and I heard the crunch of hurried footsteps on the gravel outside. Alarmed, I rushed into the hall, then straight to the kitchen. The light over the sink glowed, and an eerie quiet inhabited the room. An empty bottle of whiskey rested on the counter. I stood stock-still and listened, my senses hunting for anything out of the ordinary. The faint smell of jasmine lingered in the air.

Without warning, a distant gunshot, maybe two, blasted through the silence, and I peered out the window. The faint light of dawn had not yet arrived, and my eyes saw nothing but my reflection and blackness as I strained to capture the slightest movement.

Now fully awake, I turned back to the living room and saw

Grandpa slouched in his chair. His pale, motionless features resembled stone. I crept toward him, wondering if the noises had startled him, too. When I got closer, I stared in disbelief at the figure in front of me. I had never seen a dead body before, and I didn't need to touch him to know his skin felt cold.

Tears welled up in my eyes when I saw the empty plastic bag next to him. I knew just days ago it contained five painkillers that I bought from Eric. After Grandpa asked me to get him some, I called my old friend and explained the situation. Not that he cared, but I told Eric my grandfather needed the morphine, and I had money to pay for it. When I handed them to Grandpa the other night, he thanked me and tucked the small bag into his shirt pocket.

"Let's keep this between you and me, okay?"

"Sure Grandpa."

We didn't speak of it after that, and I never saw the pills again.

As I stood staring at my Grandpa's lifeless body, I felt a sudden urge to get rid of that bag. I snatched it from the table and as I turned away, I noticed a small latex glove on the floor next to his chair. I didn't recall seeing anything like that in the house, and something compelled me to pick it up, too. As I pondered the best way to dispose of them, I knew to avoid the trash bin. Instead, I flushed them both down the toilet.

In the bathroom, I observed the bloody towels I used for Grandpa's head wound the night before. The dried red splotches looked like morbid paint on the pastel cotton, tainted bandages from a fatal war wound. In a panic, I thought about burning them outside, but worried the smell of smoke might alert a neighbor. Instead, I fled outside, seizing the empty whiskey bottle on the way. After running to the edge of the yard, I threw the glass with all my strength, watching it disappear into the trees. With a shovel, I buried the towels deep in the dirt, returning some of Grandpa's life force to the earth.

After saying a short prayer, I returned the shovel to the shed, and hurried back inside. The house remained quiet, and I found myself alone with a corpse. Not knowing what to do, I grabbed the old telephone and dialed 911.

CHAPTER 39
NOW

C *an you describe your life in three words?* I thought about that as I hugged my mom and contemplated Grandpa's death. With the inheritance, we could live comfortably, and I would never feel bored because of my renewed love for the outdoors, especially for fishing and gardening. But I couldn't help but wonder if I'd always feel alone.

As my mom and I stare at the ocean and listen to the seagulls squawk, she doesn't ask for details about the pills I got for Grandpa. She doesn't dwell on the knowledge that I caused his death. She doesn't remind me that the police may continue their investigation. She simply keeps her arms around me.

After a time, we drift apart, and I dry my tears on my sleeve. I feel drained of emotion, like an empty vessel discarded on the beach. I'm ready to return to the car for our drive home when my mom turns to me.

"I have something I need to tell you."

I look at her and she retrieves a small flask from her pocket, unscrews the cap, pours the contents into her mouth, and swallows. Before I can reply, she starts speaking.

"I was with Grandpa the morning he died," she says softly, her voice trembling, unsure about whether to continue. "Grandpa had a dreadful type of cancer called mesothelioma, and like he said in his message to Earl, he wanted to die. He planned to end his life. We had talked on the phone a few times during his final days, and when you called me about his head injury, I knew it was time to act. I went to assist him and stay with him until the end."

My jaw drops open, but no sound emerges. Before I can even breathe or think or respond, Mom continues, the words spilling out of her like water rushing over the falls.

"I injected him with a powerful painkiller and sat with him so he wouldn't be alone. I must have fallen asleep, but when I woke up, I used the bathroom and heard someone in the house. It was you in your room, but I had been drinking. I panicked and ran out the door. I raced through the woods, back to Earl's place where I had left my car. He was up early preparing for a hunting trip."

I'm shocked. She glances at me through bloodshot eyes and drops her head into her hands. I continue staring in disbelief before I find my voice again.

"Why didn't you tell me?"

"I wanted to. I was ashamed and worried it would remind you of your dad."

"Really? They're not the same."

"But they're both suicides."

"Geez, Mom! I'm not a kid anymore. I knew Grandpa was really sick."

"It was stupid not to tell you. I thought I would come over and be gone in less than an hour. I didn't anticipate falling asleep."

"Unbelievable."

"I'm sorry."

"How could you keep that from me?"

"I don't know. It hasn't been easy. I wanted to tell you."

"What happened to honesty?"

"I guess I got scared."

"Yeah, me, too. Especially when I was in jail."

I'm somewhat relieved to learn I didn't kill Grandpa, but distressed by the knowledge that my mom did.

"Nash, I didn't think you'd call the police. I thought you'd call me, and we would report Grandpa's death together. What were you thinking?"

"You keep asking me that, and I don't know. When you wake up and someone is dead, you call the police. What were *you* thinking?"

"I thought I had it all worked out and you'd call me."

"Well, I guess you should've stayed."

"I know that now. I should've stayed and talked to you about it that morning, or maybe we should have talked about it the night before. I thought I was protecting you."

"Yeah, some protection. I could still be in jail."

"I know. I messed up big time."

"Really big time. How could you fall asleep with Grandpa dead in his chair?"

"I don't know. I told you I had something to drink."

"I saw the bottle that morning and got rid of it for you."

"You did?"

"Yes, that's why the police didn't find it."

"Oh."

"You're welcome. Did you get drunk and pass out?"

"I'm not sure. Maybe."

"Jesus f'ing Christ. At least be honest. I'm not stupid. How else would your hair end up on the rug? You passed out on the floor."

"I feel horrible about it."

"How much have you been drinking?"

"That was the first time in a long time. I don't even remember."

"Of course you don't remember. You frickin' blacked out."

"No, I mean, I hadn't been drinking much before that night."

"But you decided to that night?"

"Yeah. I wanted to take the edge off. You know, be relaxed with Fred. It was a spur-of-the-moment thing."

"You're lying. We didn't keep alcohol in the house. You brought it with you."

My mom and I lock eyes and I can't help but frown. I knew I was right and refused to back down. She looked at her feet, then slowly raised her head.

"You're right. I brought it, but I didn't plan on drinking it."

"Let me guess. You told yourself, I'll just have one glass, but then you couldn't stop."

"Something like that. I didn't want to dirty a glass, so I just drank it from the bottle."

"Good lord!"

"I'm sorry, Nash. I'm weak. I feel terrible that you had to go through being arrested and questioned and then jail time. I should've stayed to help you. Can you forgive me? It wasn't supposed to happen like that."

"If you wake up and someone is dead, you call the police. That's common sense to me."

"I just didn't expect you to do that."

"And I can't believe you lied to the police. Really? You stopped by to visit us *all the time*?"

"I didn't say that. I said I checked in with you."

"But you never did. Not once."

"I called. That's checking in."

"But that's not what you told the police." I pause for a moment, shaking my head. I exhale a mass of sour air from my lungs and stare out at the ocean. *At least I know what happened. I know the truth.* That means something, and a calm washes over me. "It's over now. It'll be okay."

"It's not okay. It's awful. I really screwed up."

"Yeah, but at least you were helping Grandpa."

"But I almost ruined you. I would never forgive myself if that happened."

"But I'm all right. We'll get through it. Everything will be all right."

"How do you know that, Nash?"

"I don't, but I have a feeling it will. We were both trying to help."

"But by not telling you I was there, I made it worse."

"Maybe, but at least I know the truth. I can piece it together now."

"What do you mean?"

"That morning, I knew someone was there because I heard the toilet flush, and Grandpa never got up early anymore. I also heard footsteps in the house, then the front door slammed, and I detected more footsteps outside. I knew Grandpa couldn't move that quickly. When I got to the kitchen, I saw the bottle, and smelled a trace of jasmine, like the perfume you always wear. But it wasn't until I found the glove on the floor that the puzzle pieces started to fit together."

Mom hangs her head again, sobbing uncontrollably. I reach out to hold her, and she rests her head on my shoulder, clinging to me for support.

"It's all right, Mom. Let's go home."

CHAPTER 40
THEN

"911, what's your emergency?"

"I need help. I think my grandpa is dead."

"I can barely hear you. Do you need help?"

"Yes. I need help!"

"Stay on the line. I can help you."

"I don't know what to do."

"Tell me what happened?"

"I think someone was here."

"Where are you?"

"I'm at home, at my grandpa's house."

"Are you there alone?"

"I don't know. I heard someone."

"What did you hear?"

"Gunshots."

"Do you have a gun?"

"No."

"Have you been shot?"

"No, but my grandpa is dead."

"I'll alert the sheriff's department. What is your address?"

"3400 Drift Creek Road."

"What city is that?"

"I don't know. It's in the forest near Drift Creek."

"What's your telephone number?"

"I don't know that, either."

"Are you calling from the emergency location?"

"Yes."

"I'll trace your call. Stay on the line."

"Okay. I'm scared."

"Try to stay calm. What's your name?"

For some reason, when I heard that question, I hung up the phone. In that moment, I wondered if I had made a mistake by calling the police.

CHAPTER 41
NOW

A somber mood follows me back to Drift Creek. There is a lot of work to do in the garden, but I've lost my enthusiasm. Grandpa and I worked on this project together, and it's not the same without him. In the next few days, I'll harvest everything I can, but toiling alone isn't nearly as much fun. I miss sharing the magic of ladybugs, butterflies, and beautiful red tomatoes. I miss him barking out orders and hovering over me, checking on my progress. And worst of all, in his absence, I'm actually going to have to clean the chicken coop.

As I stare out the kitchen window and try to motivate myself, I can't decide if it's better to stay here in isolation or return to school in Portland. My mom has to commute several hours for her hospital shifts, and she worries about leaving the house in Portland vacant too long. When she has back-to-back workdays, she stays there instead. I get it, but it means I'm left alone for days at a time.

I keep myself occupied by trying to coax the old pickup truck into starting, but it seems to have died as well. Unlike Grandpa, I'm not handy with tools, and without Wi-Fi, I can't search for any videos to help me. I know if we stay here the rest of the year, I can't survive without internet service.

A local teacher calls me one day to review my academic record. "Hi, is this Nash?"

"Yeah, hi."

"This is Michael Hayes. I can help you get on track for the GED tests."

"Okay. What do I need to do?"

"There are five sections to the exam: reading, writing, social studies, science, and math."

"How do I study for those?"

"We can meet in person or you can review the material online."

"I don't have a car right now, and my house doesn't have internet service. At least not yet."

"There is a third option then. I can mail you the materials, but you will need to show up in person to take the test."

"Yeah, okay. Mail me the stuff."

Maybe it would be simpler to reenroll in high school? I don't think so. Even though I might make some friends, I don't have enough credits to earn a diploma this year. I'd have to start junior year all over again. And I'm almost eighteen. I don't want to do that.

As I ponder my options, I crack open Grandma's recipe book, *The Joy of Cooking*. It sat on the counter all summer collecting dust, and I scan the table of contents. We have lots of eggs, and this thing called quiche sounds interesting. I can substitute a bunch of vegetables for meat, but what am I going to do about the crust? I guess I could try it without a crust, or make my own. There's a recipe for that in the book, too, but what the heck is shortening? Oh well, I'm going to attempt quiche without crust.

I spend a couple hours experimenting, then set the egg dishes aside to cool. The tops are golden brown and smell delicious, but I'll wait until my mom gets home to taste. I wander into the living room and think about reading. I can't bring myself to sit in Grandpa's chair. That was his domain. My mom doesn't sit there, either. An invisible force field surrounds it, protecting and preserving its owner's memory. I spy the backgammon board but know I'll never play without him.

I shuffle back to my room and plop onto the floor. I want to page through the photo album again and see pictures of my dad, his brother Mark, Grandma, and Grandpa. I compare them to the photos of me as a baby with my mom and dad. Everyone smiles for the camera except Grandpa. Is he unhappy or just being himself: authentic, real, and unwilling to put on a show for anyone?

The squeak of car brakes lets me know my mom is home. I head to the kitchen to meet her and help with the groceries.

"Hey, Nash. Can you get the other bags from the car?"

"I'm on it," I say, and scurry out the door.

When I return, arms loaded with paper sacks, the kitchen is empty. I figure my mom's in the bathroom, so I put away the food. I'm eager to tell her about the quiche, but she seems to have disappeared. I walk toward the bathroom to see if she's all right.

"Mom? Are you okay?"

"Yes, I'll be right out."

"Okay. I found a new recipe and made dinner."

"I'm not very hungry. Maybe you should eat without me."

"No. I haven't seen you in a couple days. Let's eat together."

"Okay. Give me a few minutes."

I return to the kitchen and make a green salad to accompany the quiche, which needs warming in the oven. When everything is ready, my mom still isn't out of the bathroom. *What can be taking so long?* I try to be patient, but I'm starving. I dish up the plates and sit down. I can't stop myself from eating. I figure I'll have a second helping when my mom gets out here. *What is going on?* After a few more minutes, I get up and walk back to the bathroom. The door remains closed, so I knock.

"Dinner is ready, Mom. Are you coming out?"

There isn't a response, so I pound on the door.

"Mom, are you okay? It's time to eat."

"Yeah, sorry."

I hear the toilet flush and the water in the sink.

"Hurry up because the food is getting cold."

When my mom opens the bathroom door, I can see it in her eyes and smell it on her breath. She was smoking a joint and drinking booze.

"What is wrong with you?" I screech. "You know that's not allowed."

"What do you mean?"

"I can smell it, Mom. You've been smoking and drinking."

"I just needed to relax a little bit. I'm exhausted from work."

"But we're not supposed to have any of that shit in the house. We're staying sober."

"It was just this once. I was getting rid of it."

"I don't know if I can believe you."

"Believe me. It was just a little, and it's gone."

I stare at her and shake my head then sit down at the kitchen table. We eat in silence at first. I can tell my mom is out of it, and I'm confused by her behavior, but I haven't had anyone to talk to all day.

"How was work?"

"It was fine, just long and tiring. Three days on is a lot in a row."

"Yeah, I bet. How's the house looking?"

"Good. A little dusty, and there are lots of cobwebs, but overall it looks okay."

"I miss my room, and the television, and an internet connection.

I'm sure you know that. Maybe we should move back there so we can take care of the house and you can be close to work? This place can survive with occasional weekend visits if we find someone to take the hens."

My mom stops eating and stares at me. I can tell she doesn't want to talk about it, but I've been thinking about it all day.

"I'm not sure that's a good idea, Nash. To put you back in that neighborhood."

"I know you're worried about it, about me. I understand, but I'm a different person now. I've changed. I'm ready to tackle my schoolwork, get a part-time job, and handle chores around the house."

"You sound pretty sure of yourself, but what happens when you run into Cecil or Eric?"

"Cecil moved, so that won't happen. And I can steer clear of Eric."

"What happens when you feel sad or bored or lonely? What will you do when you get the urge to use drugs?"

"I don't know, but with help from a therapist or a group, I think I can stay clean. I'm going to have to try at some point. I can't keep avoiding reality."

"It seems like it's too soon. With all that's happened, I don't think you're ready."

"How would you even know if I'm ready? I can't leave the house. I'm stuck here. Besides, you supposedly quit using even though you stayed in Portland with the same job and the same friends. If you can do it, why can't I?"

"It's not the same."

"Seriously? It sounds the same to me, except I won't be at school around those people. I'll study and pass the GED and stay away from Eric. I'm ready for a second chance. I'll find a job, earn some money, and get Grandpa's truck fixed. I can come here on weekends to check on the house and the garden."

"We'll talk about it later. I'm too tired right now. My head hurts. I have to clear my mind and get some sleep before making any decisions."

"Okay, but think about it. You can't keep me confined forever."

The next morning, I can tell my mom has a hangover, but I'm eager to resume our discussion about returning to Portland.

"I know you don't think it's a good idea, Mom, but being alone here all the time isn't good, either. It's driving me crazy. I feel trapped."

"I understand, but I don't think you're ready to be back in that environment."

"I am ready. I can do it. I'm going to have to try at some point, right? So why not now?"

"Now is too soon, Nash. It's just too soon. I wish I could stay here with you every day, but I have to go to work."

"I know that. I'm not an idiot. That's why Portland makes more sense! You can be at work in twenty minutes. I wouldn't be alone all the time. We would see each other more often."

"I don't know about that. It sounds good, but I worry that you'll make bad decisions and end up in trouble again."

"You're not listening to me, Mom. You never listen! I can't wait until I'm eighteen. Then I can do what I want."

I let the words hang in the air between us, then stomp out the door. I have to get out of here before I punch another hole in the wall. *She won't listen to reason.* I grab Grandpa's old hat and my fishing gear and follow the path at the far end of the yard. The bright sun, chirping birds, and buzzing insects welcome me outside. It's a beautiful day, and I should be happy, but I'm frustrated and need to escape the confines of the house. If I think it through, maybe I can convince my mom that I'm capable of staying out of trouble.

When I get to the creek, I rest on a flat rock and prepare my line. I thread the bait needle through a pink steely worm and tie the hook. The breeze feels warm on my face as I walk upstream along the bank, listening to the gurgling water. I hunt for a place to cast my line, stepping around the slippery rocks and damp earth. I stop to admire the view, smelling the sweet scent of pine. The clear water flows slower as autumn approaches, and I'll need to be patient with my line. Grandpa favored this spot, so I think I'll give it a try.

I'm grateful he reintroduced me to fishing. It's challenging, but tranquil. And although I'm secluded, I don't feel alone by the river. I can hear Grandpa's voice like I do when I'm in the garden. He's watching over me, guiding me, encouraging me to do my best. And maybe he can hear my unspoken thoughts and prayers.

I'm so distracted by memories of Grandpa that I almost drop my rod when I feel the sharp tug on my line. I quickly pull up and wind the reel. The tension on the other end tells me there is a good-sized fish on the hook. I continue my movements as I creep toward my catch with a net at the ready. The fish struggles against the line, thrashing and wriggling to get free. When I'm close and have my feet stabilized, I grab the net and scoop the creature up. It's a steelhead, more than a foot long, with iridescent pink and green scales. It looks at me with bulging eyes and a gaping mouth.

Although the prospect of having fresh fish for dinner is tempting, I decide to remove the hook and set it free. We have plenty of food in the house, and I'm not ready to take a young, vigorous life. As it swims away to the safety of the far bank, a wave of peace washes over me. *Did you see that Grandpa? I learned from the master.*

Later, when I return to the house, I can't wait to tell my mom about the fish. As I stride across the yard, I'm surprised to see a sheriff's car waiting in the gravel driveway. *Oh shit. What now?* My heart gallops, and I contemplate disappearing into the woods, back down to the creek. But I haven't done anything wrong, so I calm myself and climb the steps to the door. When I open it, I see two men seated at the kitchen table wearing uniforms. Startled by my sudden appearance, they stand when I enter.

"Are you Nash Atherton?"

"Yeah. Who are you?"

"I'm Detective Flores, and this is Detective Williams."

"What are you doing here? Where's my mom?"

"You're under arrest for conspiracy to murder Fredrick Atherton."

"What? I didn't kill anyone."

"You have the right to remain silent."

"Where is my mom?"

"Anything you say can and will be used against you in a court of law."

"Did you take my mom?"

"You have the right to an attorney."

"I know my rights! Where is my mom?"

"She was arrested an hour ago. She's been taken to the station."

CHAPTER 42
THEN

F ear gripped me in a vice after I hung up the phone. Had I just made the biggest mistake of my life? It was little consolation to know that calling for help was the right thing to do. That's what you did when someone was injured or dead. But was it a wise decision?

I paced back and forth in the kitchen, trying to think straight. I was pretty sure that Grandpa was dead. He didn't move or breathe or respond to my voice. I didn't touch him, but his pale, waxy skin looked lifeless. But what if he was still alive? He would need immediate medical attention, so getting help was logical. But I cut the call short. Would they send someone anyway?

I stopped pacing when I began to feel dizzy. *How many minutes have passed? How long do I have until the police arrive?* Not many, because moments later I heard the sirens in the distance. They were coming for me, like predators for prey. I would stay with Grandpa and meet my fate. They would point guns at me and handcuff me. They would ask me how Grandpa died. I knew it was best to say nothing, or as little as possible. I would tell them I woke up and found him dead in the chair.

CHAPTER 43
NOW

O nce again, I find myself handcuffed in the back of a squad car. It feels like a repeat of my previous nightmare: mug shots, fingerprints, alone in a holding cell wearing slippers. I know to keep quiet and not answer any questions. Thankfully, Andrea is on the way. She'll know what to do and how to help me.

As I drop myself onto the cold metal bench and lean against the green tile wall, I try to understand how I got to this point. They arrested me for conspiracy, but what does that mean? I've heard the word before, on the news or online when I learned about the assassination of JFK. Andrea will explain it; I just have to wait.

When I hear the keys jingling down the hall, I know it means food or a visitor. Although I'm hungry, I hope it's the latter. Olvera appears and frees the lock, motioning for me to follow him. We don't speak, because I know where to go. This means Andrea is here, and it raises my spirits out of the dumps.

"Hi, Nash. Are you doing okay?"

"I'm so glad you're here. I can't believe this is happening."

"They uncovered new evidence in the case. You need to tell me what happened."

"I went fishing this morning and came back to the house for lunch. Two cops were there waiting, and they arrested me for conspiracy. They said they arrested my mom, too."

"Yes, I know that. You told me all that on the phone. I mean what happened when your grandfather died?"

"Oh, then," I say, sitting down on the nearest chair.

"Yes, then. I don't think you told me the whole story."

"I didn't? Well, it's pretty simple. I woke up early because I thought I heard noises in the house. When I got out to the living room, I didn't see anyone except Grandpa, who was dead in his chair."

"And the cut on his head?"

"You know. Grandpa fell and hit his head after dinner the night before. He had used the bathroom and stumbled or something. I didn't see it, but I heard it from the kitchen. I helped him to his chair and tried to stop the bleeding."

"What did you do then?"

"I called my mom because I thought he had a concussion and needed to go to the ER. She told me to keep him awake, so I stayed up and talked to him awhile. He didn't want to go to the doctor. Before I went to bed, he asked me to get him a glass of water. Then I went to bed; that's it."

"Hmm. Okay. We'll have to wait and see what new evidence they found. I know they were looking into the medications found in his bloodstream since the autopsy report stated he died from an overdose. But only one of the medications was prescribed to him."

"Why did they arrest me and my mom? Is that the conspiracy?"

"A conspiracy means an agreement between two or more persons to commit a crime. For some reason, they think they can link both of you to your grandfather's death."

"That sounds serious."

I slump down in the chair, letting my face rest in my hands.

It was bad when I was accused of a crime, but it's terrible that my mom has been arrested, too. She'll lose her job and we'll lose the house in Portland.

"Our best defense is to show there was no agreement between you and your mom. If they can't prove an agreement to commit an offense, there is no conspiracy."

"My mom and I didn't agree on anything. As I said, we talked the night before Grandpa died, but we talked about how to treat a concussion and keep him alive."

A sharp knock on the door interrupts our conversation, and Olvera enters. He's got a sandwich and fruit for me. Andrea excuses herself and says she'll be back in an hour. Olvera escorts me back to my cell so I can eat lunch alone.

When she returns, Andrea holds a new file folder. I take a seat and brace myself for what it contains.

"There are three new items of evidence that prompted your arrest. Are you ready to hear them?"

"Yeah. Go ahead."

"The first regards telephone records. They made a note of all the calls between the house and your mom."

"Is that bad? It's pretty normal for a kid to talk to his mom."

"I agree, especially since you were spending the summer away."

"Did they record the conversations?"

"No, they didn't have any reason to believe a crime was being planned at the time. It just lists the dates, times and length of the phone calls."

"That seems easy to explain."

"Yes, circumstantial evidence, but the calls from your cell phone are different."

"They looked at those, too?"

"Yes. They pinpoint several calls between you and someone named Eric Underwood. He was arrested several days ago on charges of illegal possession and distribution of narcotics."

"Oh frick! Not Eric."

"You know Eric?"

"He's my best friend."

"Your best friend is a drug dealer?"

"No, I mean he *was* my best friend, but not since I moved in with Grandpa. Eric was involved in the April incident that's part of my arrest record."

"Ah yes, I remember: him and someone named Cecil. So that's circumstantial evidence that you were in touch with or talked to him. It's a small problem and only suggests a relationship or connection. It becomes a much bigger problem if he tells the police he sold you drugs."

"No. Eric wouldn't do that. He wouldn't tell them."

"He might if he has something tell. Or he might lie to cut a deal and save his own skin."

"I don't think he'd do that."

"But you were in touch with him. What did you talk about if you're not friends anymore?"

"Um. I don't know, stuff."

"Stuff?"

"Yeah, like what's going on in the neighborhood. What other friends are doing."

"You didn't buy drugs from him, did you?"

"Does it matter?"

"Yes, if you're put under oath and asked to tell the truth."

"Oh crap. If you have to know, then yes, I bought some, but only because Grandpa asked me to."

"Wait. Your grandfather asked you to buy him drugs?"

"He wanted painkillers. I thought it was for pain, but remember the message on Earl's machine? I think that's what he wanted them for."

"Oh shit. Okay. You might as well tell me then. What exactly did you buy?"

"Morphine."

"In what, pills?"

"Yes, five of the two hundred milligram tablets."

"Interesting, but let's put that aside for the moment. The toxicology lab found many narcotics in your grandfather's body. Besides the barbiturates and THC, one substance was an opiate and the other an opioid. No surprise, one was morphine. The other was fentanyl. The morphine was mainly concentrated in the gut and according to the medical examiner, didn't have enough time to absorb into the body before death. Morphine was not the primary cause of death."

"Is that good news?"

"In your case, yes. It was the fentanyl that killed him."

"What's fentanyl? I've never heard of it."

"It's a synthetic opioid that is much more powerful than morphine. It's typically administered using a skin patch or a needle but can also be in pill form. And that's the third piece of evidence. A second examination of your grandfather's body showed a needle mark on his right arm."

"Grandpa had been to the doctor recently."

"How long before his death?"

"I'm not sure. Maybe two weeks before."

"It could be from that, but I doubt it. The location wasn't typical for a blood draw or standard inoculation."

"I don't know what that means."

"I didn't think so, but I'm guessing that's why they arrested your mom. She's a nurse. She would know things like that and might have access to those kinds of drugs."

"They think my mom did it? She needs help! Can you help her?"

"She needs her own lawyer. I can't represent you both. It's a conflict of interest."

"Can I talk to her then? I have to talk to her."

"Not while you're being held before arraignment, but maybe after release on bond."

"It's really important, though. I need to talk to her."

"I don't think it's a good idea to talk to her about the case. We need to do what's best for you and your defense."

"But we can help her. She needs to know our plan."

"No, Nash, what she needs is a really good lawyer."

CHAPTER 44

THEN

The trees bore witness as I stood in the rain with the cops and their badges, guns, and litany of questions. I was scared stiff, afraid of saying nothing, afraid of saying too much. I don't remember how long we remained there. I just knew I felt guilty, like I'd done something terribly wrong, even though I'd only done what Grandpa had asked.

He didn't like doctors, didn't trust them he said.

"They'll keep ordering tests and prescribing pills, even if they know it won't work."

"But they're trying to help you."

"I'm beyond help."

"Please don't give up, Grandpa."

"It's time for me to go meet Helen."

"Don't say that. I need you here."

"You're a young man now. I feel comfortable leaving you in charge."

"But I can't do it alone. I need you."

"I appreciate that, but a man knows when it's time to surrender."

He thought he knew more about his own mind and body than they did. Maybe he was right, but I'm sure Dr. Baker would have prescribed him painkillers if he had asked.

When Grandpa told me he wanted to end it, I wasn't sure if he meant end his pain or his life. Or, maybe I didn't want to know. The brain has a funny way of twisting words around, bending them to meet specific needs. At the time, I had focused on what he wanted from me, not what he wanted for himself.

Our conversation seemed ominous, but not hopeless. I thought I could talk him into seeing another doctor or trying a different treatment, but when he refused to talk to me, I sensed he was in danger. Only when I heard his voice on Earl's answering machine did Grandpa's intentions become clear.

CHAPTER 45
NOW

I spend another night at the courthouse jail. During the move, I peer into every cell and open door, looking for my mom, hoping to get a glimpse of her, but I know it's futile. There are no women here. Only men and animals, and boys like me who don't fit either category. I want to tell my mom not to worry, that I'm all right. That we'll work it out. Maybe we can talk after the arraignment and come up with a plan. I imagine she'll be reduced to a puddle of tears.

When Andrea arrives, she looks professional in her navy blue suit and her hair swept up in a bun. I feel the nerves like a jackhammer in my stomach, but try to quiet them. We don't have much to discuss because we've been here before. I know to keep my mouth shut, look innocent, and say the words "not guilty" when asked by the judge.

"Hi, Nash. Did you get any sleep last night?"

"Not really. I'm so worried about my mom. In my dreams, I kept searching for her and calling for her, but I never found her. Does she know I was arrested, too?"

"Yes, I think she knows that."

"Have you seen her?"

"No, but I saw her name on the hearing docket, right before yours."

"Does she have a lawyer?"

"Stan Woodbridge. He's from Portland and is a top-notch criminal attorney."

"Okay, that makes me feel a little better."

A solid knock on the door alerts us that the judge is ready, and once again we walk into the humble courtroom. I survey the space for my mom, but she's not here yet. Andrea and I take our places at an empty table near the back, and I notice McCormack glaring at me with a smug smirk. I look him in the eye for a moment and then turn away, staring straight ahead at nothing in particular.

A few minutes later, another side door opens, and the bailiff appears with my mom and her lawyer. Stan Woodbridge is short and bald. He wears a pinstripe suit with a pocket square. Wire-rimmed spectacles perch near the end of his nose. My mom looks nervous and frightened, but finds my eyes and gives me a weak smile. When they approach the table in front me, I want to speak to her, but there isn't time.

"All rise, the Honorable Judge Abner Stevenson presiding."

We stand as the judge enters in his black robe and takes his place at the front of the room.

"Be seated. I understand there are two matters before the court today. Who is present?"

"Your Honor, it's Kent McCormack from the district attorney's office."

"Hello, Your Honor. Stan Woodbridge for the defendant Kimberly Atherton."

"Andrea Salvo for the defendant Nash Atherton, Your Honor."

"Thank you, everyone. With respect to Kimberly Atherton, does the district attorney have a criminal complaint?"

"Yes, Your Honor. Our office is prepared to charge Kimberly Atherton with second degree manslaughter in the death of Fredrick Atherton."

Wait, what? She's not being charged with murder? I can only see my mom from the back, but I notice her shoulders droop and her head hangs forward. I feel her pain, but I'm confused. I turn and look at Andrea, and she has a puzzled look on her face. My mom and her attorney lean toward each other and whisper. My mom nods her head and presses a tissue to her eyes. The air feels thick with apprehension.

"Is the defendant prepared to enter a plea?"

"Yes, Your Honor," says Mr. Woodbridge as he stands. "The defendant pleads guilty to the charge."

"No! Mom, you can't plead guilty!"

"Quiet, Mr. Atherton. It's not your turn to speak."

Andrea tugs on my arm to sit down, but I'm too upset to heed her. I pound on the table with my fists until they ache. *My mom is sacrificing herself for me. She can't do that.*

"Control yourself, Mr. Atherton, or I'll have you removed!"

Andrea pulls me down onto the chair and tears flood my eyes.

"Ms. Atherton," says Judge Stevenson. "Have you discussed this with your attorney? You're pleading guilty to a Class B felony. Do you understand the consequences?"

"Yes, we discussed it, and I understand. I signed a sworn statement about what happened."

"Mr. McCormack, the defendant was arrested for murder, but you've agreed to accept a plea to a lesser charge in this case?"

"Yes, Your Honor. We reached a deal with the defendant. She agreed to plead guilty to second degree manslaughter and serve the maximum sentence if the charges against Nash Atherton were dropped."

"Will the defendant please read the statement for the court, so it becomes part of the judicial record?"

My mom can't do this. It's crazy. She doesn't have to. It's suicide. I close my eyes as my mom speaks.

"My father-in-law, Fredrick Atherton, was terminally ill and had only weeks to live. Rather than continue to suffer from constant, debilitating pain, he asked me to assist him in committing suicide. Just before midnight on August seventeenth, I met Fred at his home located at 3400 Drift Creek Road. I brought morphine pills and a syringe with fentanyl. When he was comfortable in his chair and ready to say goodbye, he ingested the morphine pills, and I injected the fentanyl into his right arm. He passed away very soon after that. I stayed with him for an hour or so, then left the house. My son Nash, who was asleep in a bedroom with the door closed, knew nothing about my presence or his grandfather's plan to end his own life."

"Thank you. This court accepts the plea bargain and orders Kimberly Atherton to be held in custody without bail until sentencing."

What am I going to do? My mom is stuck in jail. She'll lose her job. The bank will take the house in Portland. This is horrible.

"Mr. McCormack, does the district attorney's office have another criminal charge?"

"No, Your Honor. Nash Atherton will not be charged."

"Okay. Mr. Atherton, your record will be cleared of this arrest. You are free to go."

When the gavel drops, I leap from my seat, hoping for the opportunity to hug my mom. This might be our last chance. Who knows how long she'll be in prison.

"What were you thinking, Mom? We're supposed to stick together."

"I know Nash, but it's better this way. You're doing such a great job staying sober, and I've slipped."

"I thought so, but I can help you. We can help each other."

"I'm dragging you down. You're better off without me."

"No, I don't believe that. You can't believe that."

"You'll be eighteen soon, and you can start your life over again."

"But what will I do? Where will I go? How will I make it without you?"

"You'll find a way. Listen to Grandpa. He said it best. You're a smart, strong and resilient young man."

I hug my mom one last time, then let her go as the bailiff leads her out of the courtroom. Once again, I feel abandoned by the people I love the most. *Why does this keep happening?* As I stand there, head down, tears pooling in my eyes, I sense Andrea next to me.

"You're going to be all right, Nash. It won't be easy, but I'll help you."

"Thanks. I don't know what to do."

"Come with me to my office. We can discuss your options."

CHAPTER 46
END

In Andrea's office, she asks me whether I would like to petition the court for emancipated minor status or seek a guardian to care for me.

"I don't know. Which is better?"

"It's not necessarily a matter of better, but what's more practical for you."

"Okay. What's the difference?"

"When is your birthday again?"

"February twelfth."

"That's about five months away. You'll be eighteen, right?"

"Yes."

"If you want to file a petition for emancipation, you'll need to have a place to live, means to support yourself, and submit a statement about why you want emancipation."

"I can live at our house in Portland."

"How will you pay the mortgage every month or buy food?"

"I'm not sure, but Grandpa left me property and savings in his will."

"True, but that's going to take some time to sort out. You'll need help submitting the will for probate and proving its validity.

Probate is a complex process, and involves the court, payment of debts, taxes, and distribution of assets. A minor can't be in charge of all that."

"I don't understand most of what you just said, so maybe I shouldn't seek emancipation?"

"Maybe. At some point, you'll have to deal with the probate process, but handling that at seventeen while trying to live on your own and get your GED might be too much."

"What's my other option, then?"

"Finding someone who can act as a legal guardian for you. That person steps into the shoes of a parent, helping you manage your living situation, and when you're ready, guiding you through probate."

"That sounds good, but who would do that for me?"

"Do you have any other relatives? Aunts, uncles, cousins?"

"I don't think so. I've never met any."

"What about your other grandparents? Kimberly's parents. I remember talking to her briefly about her side of the family before your initial arraignment."

"Mom never talked about them. She said they lived in a hick town out east. I'm not sure where, and I barely remember meeting them. I think I did once when I was five or six."

"Okay. In a few days you'll be able to visit your mom in jail, and maybe you can ask her about them. In the meantime, what are you going to do?"

"I don't know. If I get a ride back to Drift Creek, I can drive my mom's car to Portland. I can look through her stuff at the house and try to find some names, a phone number, or something."

"That's a good idea. I'll get you to Drift Creek, and we'll stay in touch."

When I unlock the bungalow door in Portland and step inside, a musty smell fills my nostrils. The house is quiet, and I tiptoe across the room so I don't disturb the sofa, lamp, and end table. I proceed to the kitchen, surveying the empty counters, then opening the refrigerator. A moldy loaf of bread, two rubbery-looking apples, and some half-empty condiment jars stare back at me. I shut the door and head for my room. A magnetic force pulls me to the bed, and I fall onto it, face first. *Oh, how I missed my bed.* I suddenly love its lumpy mattress, flattened pillow, and mismatched sheets.

I must have fallen asleep, because it's dark when I wake up. I hurry to the bathroom to relieve myself, then feel the pangs of hunger claw at my empty belly. After gathering all the loose change around the house, and finding a bit more in the car, I drive to Taco Bell for a feast.

Back home, I open all the drawers in the kitchen looking for paperwork about the house, my mom, or anything that might help me. When I come up empty, I go to my mom's bedroom. *She's got to keep that stuff somewhere.* As I search through more drawers, I find an unopened bottle of whiskey. I'm caught for a second, frozen in a parallel moment back when I discovered the booze at Grandpa's. But this time is different. I grab the bottle and head for the kitchen. I unscrew the cap and pour the contents into the sink, watching it disappear down the drain.

I resume my search in her closet, and there I find a sturdy file box hidden beneath a pile of sweaters. Lifting the lid, I see a row of neatly labeled files: Birth, Diploma, Loan, Marriage, Mortgage, Name, Photos, Social Security. I select the one labeled for photos and remove it from the box. As I shuffle through the prints like a deck of cards, I realize I don't recognize anyone. Some of them have dates written on the back, but others are blank. One of the girls looks like my mom, but I'm not certain, so I set the pictures aside.

I grab another file and discover a birth certificate for Kimbelle Joy Riser. She has the same birthdate as my mom, and her parents are Albert and Maybelle Riser. *Is this my mom? Did she change her name?* I reach for the file marked "Name" and learn the truth. My mom changed her name to Kimberly Rise when she turned eighteen. I want to confirm this, so I reach into the box to find her high school diploma. It says Kimbelle J. Riser, but her nursing degree says Kimberly J. Rise.

Several days later, I visit my mom in jail and bring some of the photos with me. We hug and sit down at a modular table in the corner of the room.

"It's good to see you, Mom. Are you doing okay?"

"I'm doing fine, honey. What about you? You look good."

"I am good, I think. I have to tell you, though, that I took the cash from your file box. I needed it to buy food and gas."

"My file box? You've been in Portland. I was thinking you would be at Drift Creek, but that's fine. I'm glad you found it. I was saving it for an emergency, and I guess this qualifies."

"Yeah, it does. Since we only have thirty minutes, I need to ask you about these photos. Who are these people?"

I spread them out on the table in front of us like a puzzle. She gazes at them in silence, picking them up and putting them down, one by one.

"They're my family. You only met them once."

"I thought so. I was pretty young, but I sort of remember. Is this you?"

"Yes, that's me, with my parents and Kevin."

"How old were you? There's no date on the back."

"I think I was nine."

"Is Kevin your brother?"

"Yes. He's nine years older than me, and he was leaving for college. I didn't really know him. He was like another parent."

"Do you know where he lives?"

"I'm not sure, but I have a phone number from when he lived in Eugene. It might be old, but it's written on the inside of file marked 'Birth.'"

"Okay. I'll look for that when I get home."

"Do you plan to call him?"

"Yes. Andrea thinks I need a guardian. Someone who can act like a parent, and help me get on my feet, at least until I'm eighteen. A guardian could also handle the probate of Grandpa's will."

"Right. You can't do those things until you're officially an adult."

"And it sounds too confusing anyway: courts and taxes and distributions. I want to be working and studying for the GED."

"Good. I'm glad you're still focused on that."

"Yeah. It's gonna be tough, but I can do it."

"I know you can."

"So if I call Kevin, will he know I exist?"

"Yes, of course, Kevin knows he's an uncle. He met you when you were a baby, but then he did a lot of traveling and lived abroad for several years. We lost touch, but I know he visits our parents, so if you had to locate him that way, you could find the Risers in Rufus."

"The what?"

"Risers, our last name. They live in Rufus, Oregon. It's out east on the Columbia."

I pause for a moment and a million thoughts run through my head.

"How come you don't talk to your parents?"

"Wow, that's a heavy question. It's complicated."

"Try me."

"Okay. Here it is. I moved to Portland as soon as I graduated from high school. I had to get away from them and that hick town. They were pretty upset, telling me if I left I shouldn't bother coming back. I thought about following Kevin, but I didn't want him stuck in the middle. You probably saw it in the file. I changed my name as soon as I could, then got a job, took out a student loan, and started college."

"That's pretty brave of you. How did Dad fit into all this?"

"I met him in Portland and we fell in love. When I got pregnant with you, we decided to get married. I invited my folks to the wedding, but when they found out I was already knocked up, they told me I wasn't their daughter. Thankfully, Jeff's parents were open to the marriage. Fred and Helen were so great. They accepted me as their daughter. And they helped us financially so I could continue with school and get my degree."

"Wow. That sounds hard. And my being around made it worse."

"Don't you ever say that Nash. Your dad and I wanted a child. I can't speak for Jeff, but you are the bright spot in my life. You always have been. I know it doesn't seem like it lately, but I love you. I just got way off track and wasn't thinking clearly. I'm sorry."

"It's okay, Mom. We're getting back on track."

"Well, I'm going to get clean now and stay that way. No more drugs. No more booze. No more lying. I'll get a second chance, but it might not be for a long time."

"Do you know when the sentencing hearing is? I want to be there."

"It's November nineteenth. My lawyer is going to ask for leniency because Grandpa wanted to die and he only had a short time left in this world, but I'm prepared to do the ten-year maximum."

"Ten years? Geez, that's a long time."

"Yeah. You'll be twenty-seven when I get out. I think it comes with a hefty fine, too. Maybe two hundred fifty thousand dollars? I'll have to sell the house to pay that."

"Really? That sucks. You'll be starting over."

"It's the punishment for making big mistakes. At least you're in the clear. When you turn eighteen, your juvenile record will be sealed. Nobody has to know."

We stare at each other for a few moments, neither of us knowing what to say.

"I have to go, Mom. Visiting time is over."

"Will you come again soon?"

"Of course. I'll be here next week."

We stand and hug, then walk toward the exits. Mom uses the door on the left, which leads to the cellblock. She turns and gives me a weak smile before disappearing. I follow the path to the right, walking outside to freedom.

ABOUT THE AUTHOR

Ann Worthington is a retired lawyer and mother of two who lives in Southern California. When she's not reading or writing, she's walking on the beach, swimming, or playing pickleball. This is her first novel. You can find more of her work at www.annworthington.com.

In this age of social media sharing, without social proof, an author may as well be invisible.

So if you've enjoyed *Tales of Nash*, please consider giving it some visibility by reviewing it on Amazon or Goodreads. A review doesn't have to be a long critical essay. Just a few words expressing your thoughts, which could help potential readers decide whether they would enjoy it, too.

CPSIA information can be obtained
at www.ICGtesting.com
Printed in the USA
LVHW092132210720
661248LV00001B/110